RICHARD CURREY'S

THE WARS OF HEAVEN

"*The Wars of Heaven* is a beautiful book....Currey is a colorful and poetic writer, a painter of startling yet flowing images. Both his tragic and comic figures are created with a compassionate hand that is too rare in fiction these days. More than half the book is a delightful, picaresque novella, whose central character Delbert Keene's comically heroic adventures are not unlike those of one Huck Finn....It is not hyperbole to call him a lasting contribution to American literature." —*Seattle Post-Intelligencer*

"Richard Currey has staked out the dream side of reality.... The inspired novella ["The Love of A Good Woman"] that caps *The Wars of Heaven* is hilarious in a big way, but also tender, wise, and challenging. It is a headlong romp, a plunge, an all-out assault on stuffiness and sobriety...a seamless delight." —*Los Angeles Times Book Review*

"In *The Wars of Heaven*, Currey renders a series of exquisitely melancholy images...with the authenticity and pathos of vintage photographs. These characters are limned with compassion and sensitivity....Currey's is an eloquent voice." —*Publishers Weekly*

"Beautiful, haunting, and poetic...Through sensitive characterizations and a humane, heart-piercing understanding, Richard Currey unravels tales that harbor a depth steeped in the colors of the human spirit." —*Columbus Dispatch*

Books by Richard Currey

FATAL LIGHT
THE WARS OF HEAVEN

THE
WARS
OF
HEAVEN

THE
WARS
OF
HEAVEN

———

RICHARD CURREY

VINTAGE CONTEMPORARIES
VINTAGE BOOKS
A DIVISION OF RANDOM HOUSE, INC.
NEW YORK

FIRST VINTAGE CONTEMPORARIES EDITION, OCTOBER 1991

The stories in this collection appeared originally in *High Plains
Literary Review, The North American Review, Quarterly West, Story,*
and *Witness.* "The Wars of Heaven" also appeared in *Prize Stories 1988:
The O. Henry Awards, New American Short Stories,* and *La
Nouvelle Revue Française* (Paris). The author extends appreciation to
the editors of all these publications.

Library of Congress Cataloging-in-Publication Data
Currey, Richard, 1949–
The wars of heaven / Richard Currey.—1st Vintage contemporaries ed.
        p.   cm.—(Vintage contemporaries)
                ISBN 0-679-73465-1
                        I. Title.
        [PS3553.U6665W3   1991]
        813'.54—dc20   91-50011
                        CIP

Manufactured in the United States of America
10   9   8   7   6   5   4   3   2   1

FOR MY GRANDFATHER
EVERETT CURREY
1890–1961

Five editors were particularly important in bringing my stories to a first readership: Dominique Aury, Robert O. Greer, Jr., Gloria Norris, Peter Stine, and Robley Wilson, Jr. Their advocacy is much appreciated. I'm deeply grateful as well to Seymour Lawrence and Camille Hykes for their unstinting energy and commitment. Rob Brager's dedication to my family has my fullest gratitude. And my wife, Aiko, is everywhere in this work: her unwavering support has made all the difference.

CONTENTS

TYLER'S
BALLAD

Edward Tyler remembered his forty-first birthday: his brother came back from the woodshed but wasn't carrying any wood, and told Tyler they had better go back down to the shed together. The clouds were dark and low and against them five sparrows hobbled south toward a grove of walnut and black cherry. Rain was coming.

■　　■　　■

Edward Tyler drove the night train north from Charleston and back again, had done so since 1931, after the Depression killed the family farm and forced him into another line of work. He started as a brakeman, then fireman, made his way to engineer, loving the seasons of the night, the smell of coal smoke laced with winter and the air-through-teeth hiss of steam's release when he vented the boiler at the stations along the way. He leaned at the cab's open hatch and watched the transfer of mail and merchandise halfway down the train — silhouettes and unreadable voices — until it was quiet and the platform was empty and the brakeman's signal light sliced an arc into the darkness. Tyler pulled the throttle slowly and the engine jerked forward against the weight of the train, a muscle unfolding in a blind man's arm.

Riding through the hills and watching the rails' blue shine in starlight he would sing to himself, and his voice merged with the moan of the engine until the music was something that happened in his lingering imagination, like memory or the remnants of dream. The locomotive's headlamp wobbled a line of light in front of the cars of chickens and cabbages, refrigerator vans, flatbeds and tankers and gondolas and the endless barges of coal.

His schedule laid over in a depot town called Carneyville. Tyler and his crew crowded into the stationmaster's office, stripping their work gloves, laughing, smelling of kerosene and black coffee. Tyler sat on the leather divan talking about the prices of corn and soybeans and beef, about FDR and the New Deal. He listened to jokes about the pope and colored people and the local whores, and jokes about old men like himself who were married to beautiful young women.

■ ■ ■

Edward Tyler and Elizabeth Roman were married in a mountain church. White clapboard, one room at the end of a packed-earth lane, random tombstones climbing the hill like teeth in an old man's mouth. Not many were in attendance. A few friends, Tyler's aging mother sitting in the front pew with wildflowers on her lap. Elizabeth's father. The minister's wife playing "Amazing Grace" on a pump organ. A mongrel dog slept in the aisle.

Elizabeth seemed unbelievable to Tyler: a fragile beauty, ethereal eyes invested with a kind of elementary clarity he had never seen before. She stood so gently beside him in front of the altar, and as the preacher read from his litanies Tyler looked at Elizabeth. They had met at a Christmas dance, introduced by Elizabeth's father, a friend of Tyler's, and Tyler danced with her most of the night and took her home in the crisp mountain air, and they were married six months later. He was forty. She was twenty-two.

He rented a house outside of Charleston, the last of a farm cut down to two acres and a barn, garden plot, woodshed and root cellar. He bought a milking cow and a radio and watched Elizabeth move through the house, watched her as she slept, brought her clothes and perfume from Pittsburgh, and was gone every other week of the month driving up the green map of West Virginia.

■ ■ ■

The night of Edward Tyler's forty-first birthday it rained: he remembered it well. It was the night his brother found Elizabeth in the woodshed, where she had ended her life with a deer rifle, sitting on a box of pine chips with her eyes open, looking exhausted and melancholy, the back of her skull open and wet on the dark wood. The gun had slipped from her grip and leaned barrel-up between her legs. Her hands lay empty to either side, palms gently opened as if they might speak.

For most of three weeks Tyler sat in a single chair under a single lamp, not eating, only a distant awareness of the run of sympathetic visitors, his body fighting his mind's insistence on complete despair. He had seen no signs of trouble: Elizabeth was often silent, at times unable to sleep and drifting through the long hallways at night, but Tyler took it for diffidence and intensity — aspects of her beauty — and stared from his mourning chair cursing his ignorance and willingness to imagine an identity for a woman he did not know. He wanted to have a place for what his life had become but found none, and felt like an empty shape filling with apparitions and the soft drum of autumn rain. He would pass off to sleep sitting in the chair and start awake in the midst of nightmare, Elizabeth's corpse speaking to him from her death seat in the woodshed, her disembodied voice an emanation. Tyler gripped the chair's arms and rediscovered his face, aligned in a rigid mask of anguish and disbelief before he called himself back into being, trying to find a breath of air in the darkened room.

He wanted simply to understand, and saw that he could not, and would never.

In time he was back at work, back on his route. He moved out of the farmhouse and into a condemned caboose on a siding in the switching yards and though he had never been religious he prayed. *Jesus,* he whispered, *protect me from my innocence. Love me in my weakness.*

His train was a friend, unwinding its way out of rain-misted hills. The long stretches through the central part of the state he rode alone at the cab's window, knowing if he reached out to touch the rhododendron and chokecherry that crowded the roadbed splits his hand would be pulled into a rapture of night purple, as sweet as blood. The train would break from undergrowth and forest, and meadows would stretch away filled with moonlight and ground mist. Tyler searched for a direction he could depend on, and thought of Elizabeth. On one late winter night, as his train rounded the long bend beyond the Afton station, he found himself in tears and saying aloud *I didn't know you, girl. I didn't even know you,* his voice lost in diesel roar.

OLD FIRES

HIS NAME WAS James Heard and the distant thunder woke him: he lay awake before he knew what had drawn him up.

Then he heard it again, dark roar in the sky, the slight shock wave jetting underground behind it. He was on the side of the bed putting his socks on when his wife said something to him from her sleep and he turned to answer but saw from her face in the half-light she wouldn't hear. He got up and went to the closet and dressed in front of the closet's open door.

When he reached the porch one of the mine foremen was there, stopped on the steps carrying a Coleman lantern in his left hand, its light striking his face into shadow. The foreman stood for a moment, his lips working silently and the light spreading a wavering circle over the floorboards of the porch. There was no wind. The night was cold. The foreman shivered once and said, quietly, *You know your brother's down there tonight.* And then he looked away, from his shoes to the lantern's bright blowing hiss, turned, stepped down and moved off, lantern walking beside him until it was only a flickering point in the darkness.

■　■　■

James Heard had worked fourteen years underground, digging coal with his older brother Benjamin. They had grown up in northeastern Kentucky, around Little Crane Creek in a family of nine children. Their father was killed when his truck rolled off an iced bridge in the middle of a long winter, and Ben took over, coming home drunk after the old man's death, only seventeen at the time, their long-sick mother sitting upstairs staring from the edge of her empty bed. When she died with pneumonia in the next autumn Ben scattered the younger children to relatives but kept James with him, talked to him for weeks about leaving, north to West Virginia and the rumor of work.

James packed in the old bedroom wallpapered with *Jefferson County Democrats* — one wall dominated by FDR in dark glasses, the yellowed presidential face razored by that savage grin — and stopped on the way out to the road to pull a palm of boneset and joe-pye weed. He tossed the spray of tiny blossoms across his mother's grave behind the house. He could hear his brother calling and for a brief moment standing there at her feet he thought he could feel the land singing itself underground, an aura of rivers and trains humming inside the earth. Then Ben was beside him, saying it was time to go.

On the shoulder of the county two-lane Ben joked, did a short dance to imaginary music in his two-tone oxfords and pleated wool trousers. He adjusted the brim of his hat and leaned on his knees like an umpire, squinting into the overcast for the first car up they could hitch a ride with.

■　　■　　■

When James Heard got to the mine the main hole was bright, lit from inside and below by flame, talking fire blowing into view, wisping reds and yellows and the hollow color of peaches underneath. A smoke billow turned continuously into the belly of the night sky, its boiling flank white in the fire's light. Firemen had opened hoses full-force into the gate and down the shaft. There were wives against the fence in curlers and slippers, keening and crying; a group of older women stood back, solemn in coats over their bathrobes. James Heard pushed in close, found the foreman who had come to his house, but there was nothing to do but wait. The company wasn't exactly sure how many were down there, the foreman said. Could be near a hundred.

Heard turned back against the gathering crowd feeling his own breath coming in gusts, past faces shining in the glare, some he knew, wives and sons and daughters, brothers and fathers. He said nothing, acknowledging with nods or a touch as he passed, and stepped free of the crowd, stumbling slightly, steadying himself against the first tree he came to, a short birch, hearing his breath reach and pull and he held to it, the simple sound of it in his mind.

■ ■ ■

By dawn there was soft rain, a whisper in the surrounding forest. His wife brought coffee and sandwiches, taking up vigil with him. Some of the other wives sat on folding chairs in a half-circle, wrapped in blankets, singing cold soulful hymns and reading passages aloud from the New Testament.

It was afternoon when the foreman came to say there was no further use in waiting. The mine was still burning, the governor was sending out a special disaster team. The foreman glanced around, his cheeks sooted. *Might be days before this hole burns out*, he said.

James Heard nodded. The foreman waited a moment before he said *Jesus, Jimmy, I'm so goddamned sorry.* Heard looked at the ground. The foreman touched his arm and moved off and Heard stood, families drifting away in silence around him through the rain, until he was alone with the smoking head of the shaft. He stood watching the smoke plume and felt himself a solitary figure in a secret landscape. When he walked slowly down the slope through wet leaves to where he had parked his truck, his wife was waiting for him.

He started the engine, turned it off, sat in the worn smell of work and old oil and coal dust. His wife stared straight ahead through the windshield. Drizzle ticked on the cab's roof and he looked at his big hands resting on the steering wheel.

He started the engine a second time and took the truck home.

■　■　■

He told himself he could forget, it would pass, but sudden rages convulsed him, riveted the room and left his wife and children remote and frightened. He lost himself in tirades, came to his senses alone and confused in front of the television with the sound turned down, dancing blue light in a black corner. He lost interest in sleeping, and sat up at the kitchen table resting his head in his hands with his eyes closed, listening to the furnace under the floor rumble on and off, his face a closed and silent territory. Over and over the night fire stood in his mind and he saw the new widows along the hollow on that November dawn, looking toward the fume of greasy smoke to the east, and when he did sleep he dreamt of burning tunnels, men choking the fire-holes trying to see some pocket free of the terrible light and heat, just some place they could rest out of their pain.

His wife insisted he see a doctor for something to help him sleep and ease his nerves, but when he finally sat in the alcohol smell of the examining room he felt foolish, his brother's death only another random secret.

He made up a story about a shoulder cramp, was palpated and purged by the old doctor's cold raspy hand, told he shouldn't worry.

■　　■　　■

The state sealed the mine after two weeks and James Heard could have moved to one of the company's other sites, but he hired on with a strip-mine project, driving backhoe, shaving down the sides of mountains. He felt he couldn't go underground again. He had a morbid fantasy, a kind of daydream, that if he went below the surface he would find Ben there, that Ben haunted the earth if only for the sake of accident and loss. In better moments he was able to tell himself that this was a private fever, and sitting on his porch with a beer on a Sunday in spring he began thinking about chance, if there was such a thing, or if life had design and every moment was earned, his years the heart of some crippled innocence. He thought of his childhood in Kentucky and realized the memory he had most, he wasn't sure why, was of the first hog butchering he and Ben had seen, at least the first he remembered.

It was winter, snow-filled. Neighbors crowded the kitchen. He and Ben took turns grinding coffee beans for their mother. Some of the men held their mugs in both hands and their conversations seemed distant and muffled. The family dogs padded the kitchen sniffing bootheels. The boys' father mounted the steps and crossed the porch, his boots echoing the crawlspace, and he came through the door patting gloved hands together, into the kitchen in front of a surge of cold air. *Ready*, he called out, stamping snow from his boots on a mat, taking a cup of coffee from his wife. The other men pushed the last of their coffees down and scraped their chairs back.

James and Ben got into coats and followed the men out into the winter, crunching frost to the clearing in front of the barn. The hog rooted and snorted in a tight cage on the back of Clyde Kelley's flatbed, its breath vaporizing on the snowy air.

Clyde took his Ruger carbine off the truck's front seat, drew a single shell out of his overalls bib pocket and loaded it into the chamber, pulling the hammer back until it cocked. Two of the men moved the cage to the end of the truck's bed and Clyde pushed the rifle's barrel through the mesh and rested it against the hog's forehead. The animal blinked once, confused, and Clyde fired, at that range the shot a muffled thump into bone, and the hog's full weight slammed to the floor of the cage. Clyde withdrew the rifle, rested the barrel in the crook of his left arm and unlatched the cage door. There was a short trail of burnt cordite in the air as three of the farmers lifted the dead animal out of the cage and onto a meathook, hanging it on a crossbeam the boys' father had nailed together the night before, and Clyde opened the suspended carcass with his big serrated skinning knife, one clean draw down the midline.

■ ■ ■

After the butchering their father decapitated the hog and sunk the head in a bucket of snowmelt. It sat in a corner of the kitchen and James went to look. The hog stared up at him through empty eyes, tendrils of lacy blood oozing under the neck stump and drifting in the clear water, and he stood back in a sudden and unexpected nausea, gasping, striking a chair. His mother turned from the stove and watched a moment, said *Nothing to be afraid of son. It's just an old hog.* The hot kitchen slid in his head and he looked at her, sick and trying to speak, the same backward ache that had risen in him when Clyde ripped his knife down through the hog, throat to belly, guts sagging into the rift, blood sluice, the sound of water gushing, and James gripped his brother's hand feeling his lips pull away from his teeth, his throat contracting, frightened and not knowing why, and they stood side by side under the feral cries of crows and the wise float of hawks on the white uplifts above, the hog's opened body steaming in January air.

■　■　■

In the months after his brother's death James Heard sat at a table in his toolshed, a single plywood sheet across two sawhorses. He had tried some of his old projects — wooden toys, carvings — but they stopped halfway done. He seemed to lose their direction, as if he could no longer depend on the energy inside the wood to guide him. He started a toy truck of loblolly and spruce but now the partially carved blocks sat in front of him on the plywood sheet, refusing his hand. He leaned back and looked toward the toolshed's southern window. Under the window was a small angel he had carved, one of his oldest pieces, a polished cherry standing in a frail cone of summer light with arms and hands slightly away from the body, the three pairs of wings raised in delicate flutter. The carved angel looked quietly down at the fresh vegetables on the table, gifts from a neighbor. Bell peppers arranged at random in a geometric triad, their heavy skins shining, two zucchini squashes and a tomato to the side with cheeky bulges glowing a mild green luster from under the red. The angel gazed on the vegetables as if they were the mysterious fruits of heaven and James Heard looked at the accidental tableau feeling it nearly meant something, the way the angel's hands lifted with just the right knowledge.

With the sound of children he got up and went to the small window at the angel's head and saw his sons and their friends running the side yard. He watched them and one of the boys, Fred Chapel's son, was pushed and lost balance sideways into the Heards' garden plot, taking down a stake as he fell. The boy looked back at the house and got up dark, frightened at his trespass, fists tight and ready to swing. James Heard stepped out of the shed and let the boys see him, and said *Forget it, just go on and play somewhere else.* The boys stood, saying nothing, looking at each other, then turned to pass deeper into the yard, trotting, then running, toward the cornfields and wooded land beyond. Fred Chapel's son stood alone for a moment in a furrow, sullen and flushed, and Heard said quietly *Go on now, catch up to your buddies.*

Heard went back into the shed and racked his tools on a pegboard. He held the angel a moment in his palm. He still wondered if he could have shaped it: the eyes seemed to understand themselves beyond the carver, the way they owned their blind dreams whole. As if the angel wanted to know whose vision saw the world for it, and in whose light it went on living. James Heard wiped the dust from the wings with his thumb, buffed the backside on his trouser leg and put the angel back under the window, and went to stand in the doorway. The early summer evening was long and deep, and like a good secret the air was close, a life in itself. He stood a moment, listening to the night. Then he collected the vegetables and walked out across the yard toward his house.

BELIEVER'S
FLOOD

———

My STORY is no regal tale. Take my word for it. I sit here on this derelict front porch struggling for just one breath at a time and at sixty-two years of age I am not that old a man though my years shifting coal have rendered me such, taking my air and the kind of days I once had. I made twenty-four years underground before I strangled on the way they make the dark down there, before I was a lost soul in a glider on a summer morning waiting every day for the mailman to come, just that one extra person to talk to. Except I cannot talk, not well and not for long. I'm too busy breathing. Got my lips pursed, rounded, that's the way I was taught by the doctors up at the university, lean forward on my knees they told me, make like I'm about to whistle and let that air come short and sweet, do the least work possible keeping it there, go on and let it push itself. *Black lung. What we doctors call silicosis. What it really means is you can't breathe too well.* Which I did not need a doctor to tell me. You can sit in my shoes and feel for just one moment the pressure of unadulterated air all around you, genuine air thin as a clean knife up against your eyes and in at your throat and you'll know what I mean, you'll know how it is to be a cat on a hook and coal dust hovering in your chest like a down of rime, lungs dropsied and purple in a bed of old blood and walking away from the light. A lifetime in a coal mine frees me to this. Working a long heat wave for what I could never have, and I'm told to be happy with what it's come to. Go home at last and sit in a chair and try to breathe, testament to a lifetime's plain glory: sitting in a chair and working to draw one good breath, one decent breath, one clean and simple breath.

I am Raymond Dance, born and raised in Red Jacket, West Virginia. My father worked for the Red Jacket Consolidated Coal and Coke Company though not underground, lived what appeared to be a happy life, modest and without ceremony, straight-through and reliable. Everybody here then worked for Red Jacket Coal and Coke. The company owned the town. The storekeeper took company scrip and turned it over to a man in a tired suit who came around once a week. I remember trying to talk to my father about all of this and it's where a son hesitates, having spent so many years in the older man's shadow one way or another. You reach a point where you can't help but wonder if the old man has ever considered what you've thought about so long, what has come to dominate your way of thinking. My father never approved of my union work, never seemed to understand it or what we aimed for, and he listened silently while I told him of a battle for a better life, for wages and rights and a thimbleful of self-determination. A lofty speech.

My father grunted, glanced at me full of contempt as if he pitied me for some wholesale foolishness, got up and went inside the house, let the screen door slam behind him.

That was that. The first and last time the subject was to
come between us. We stayed friendly enough to his death.
Now I can look at the ground he's buried in and wonder why
I never got so much as a go-to-hell when I claimed that we
could someday pull out of the grip of the coal operators. When
it came to my father I was always looking for myself in the
wrong direction.

■ ■ ■

We had a movie theater in town — another thing owned and
operated by the company — that by no real shift of the tongue
could be called a theater, being an old Grange hall outfitted
with folding chairs and a whitewashed wall. They showed
movies once a week, every Friday night, and as far back as I
can recollect I was there in a hardback chair staring up into
that wall like it was heaven's gate for sure. It wasn't exactly that
I wanted to be like those people, just that I wanted to know
who they were, where they came from, what they were thinking. I suppose if I hadn't been that kind of boy I would never
have been the sort to give my father his confusions about me.
But I was that kind, edge of curiosity killing the cat and
enough imagination to always want to see how the story comes
out in the end. You have to remember these were silent pictures. Nobody played piano. The projector clicked along,
prophecy and wide-open promise, that ray of light cutting just
over my head into another life where the poor and the hopeless always managed to locate a solution of some kind, or
laughed their way through hell. The actors spoke without
making a sound, and I never saw a picture that was about
anybody I could possibly know yet I still found a comfort
there, a belief in the sanctity of what might come to pass, and

when the union organizers arrived I was ready as any man could be.

■　■　■

The mine wars were like nothing we had ever seen. God-awful, bloody, terrifying to the bone. Red Jacket Coal and Coke showed their colors well enough and just like we expected hired in hoods and killers, Baldwin-Felts detectives for the most part. We all went at each other, baseball bats and rocks and knives and finally guns. I lost teeth and busted my nose and my wife Alice was calling me off the whole affair. She reminded me there were miners who were not union: they kept clear of trouble and hoped they'd be alive and still have a job when the smoke cleared, and she was telling me to take their example, stay home and wait. But I had too much of a taste for it, I was too sure it was the right thing to do and that I couldn't live with myself if I wasn't out there in the fray, going to meetings, saying my share. I've never felt different and I've never had a regret.

There was the night me and Wilbur Landown took on three Baldwins out in the Williamson field, the two of us standing vigil on picket, thinking we had a quiet shift, an easy time of it in the middle of the night sometime in June of 1920. The scabs were inside working the mine at about a third of what a real force of men could do, but nobody had come up to the line on foot and we knew we had trouble when these three yokels sauntered out of the dark, big hats and looking like brothers on the lam from daylight. There was no conversation, no negotiating with these boys, they sauntered a while but as they came in close they started to run at us. Two of them were over me like a blanket drawn across my head, flailing, pound-

ing my chest with so much force you'd think I was carrying a
Congo gorilla on my back. I heard Wilbur screaming, and I
heard the soft grunt of fists coming into flesh and I was rolling
around, taking a bruising but the Baldwins were in too close
for real damage, more like wild boys in a schoolyard. I pulled
loose and scrabbled backward in the dirt; one old boy was
standing over me and in the downswing with a club the size
of a bull's hind leg. I got to my knees and coupled my fists and
brought my arms right up into the bastard's crotch: that stick
still hit me broadside across the shoulders but there wasn't
much punch left in the blow and my man fell down on his
butt with his hat across his eyes. I stood up and took a sucker
punch to the upper lip that knocked me straight flat; for a
minute there I didn't know a thing. I came to in a haze with
Wilbur pulling me upright. Wilbur looked in at me and his
face was the grandest goddamn mess you've ever seen: teeth
gone in front, nose bent sideways, cheeks and hair smeared
with dirty blood. He looked at me and his eyes were bright and
full of good times and he was grinning as if he'd heard the best
joke of his life. Come on, he said, let's send these fellas down
the chute. My mind wasn't any too clear and Wilbur held me
up by a shoulder, saying You don't look too good, know that?
I told him he was handsome as ever, and got to my feet. One
of the Baldwin men was gone, run off; the other two were on
the ground and for all I knew were dead. Wilbur was already
dragging one toward the mine gate, motioning me to do the
same with the other. I got my man at the ankles and pulled
him along; he started groaning and his eyes fluttered. Wilbur
pressed the elevator call switch and I heard the old metal cage
clanking up the shaft. My man said something blurred by a
mouthful of swollen tongue, tried to lift his head to no avail.

I got worried the elevator would come up filled with Baldwins and we'd be dead for sure, but the cage scraped into moonlight empty. Wilbur opened the gate, dragged in his man. I did the same, closed the gate and sent them both back down.

When I got home I told Alice we'd run into some trouble at the picket line. She dabbed my wounds and frowned, didn't ask for details.

■   ■   ■

Next morning I had Alice and the two babies with me at the train station. Alice was grim, thin-lipped; the new sky overhead was wild as fire and water and in the time we stood on the platform we didn't speak. All I wanted was to board a train with all of us in one piece.

The northbound came in and took us out and we were a good seven miles from town when Alice said we shouldn't come back. Not for a long while, she said.

I looked out the window with my older daughter on my knee. Well, I said. I'll have to come back.

Alice stared at me with a look that held every insult I could hear. After a moment she told me I was like all the rest, just a damned fool.

I was scared and empty-handed and wanting nothing more than to agree, to stay on with her family near Welton, help around her father's farm. Let it all blow over.

She asked me exactly what had happened, and I told her.

She took off her hat and pushed at her chestnut hair. They'll be waiting for you, she said.

I told her I was sure they would be.

The whistle blew as the train slammed through a water

crossing. I'll stay a spell with you at your folks' place, I said. And then I'll come back. I can't just disappear.

Alice looked at our daughters, each in turn. The baby in Alice's lap began to cry and I remember to this day the sound of that cry and the shape in Alice's eyes, washed-away, proud and cold as ice. My God, she whispered.

■　■　■

I came back into Red Jacket at dusk three days later thinking our house would be gone, burned out or vandalized. It was our own home, land that had been in my mother's family, outside town limits and it was there, still standing pretty as you please, that old coat of ivory paint peeling black under years of coal soot. They had been there, somebody had: the front door stood open. It had rained in; dead leaves blew straight into the parlor. I went through every room, every closet, cupboard, shelf. I looked under beds and up the chimney until I was satisfied nobody was waiting for me. By then it was dark, and I turned on all the lights downstairs, drew the curtains to give the place a warm and homey look from the road. I locked the front and back doors and all the windows, and took the shotgun from the hall closet corner. Upstairs I pulled off my boots and socks, loaded the gun with two shells full of number six buckshot and sat in my bedroom in the dark, shotgun in my lap, terrified of every little sound I heard. I had the time, sitting there, to think about my situation, to consider the plight of a man who dispatches his family to innocent country and sits afraid for his life in his own home simply because he wants to trade his labor for a decent wage, and the Baldwin men stepped up on the front porch. Knocked politely at the front door. I kept my seat.

I heard them speak to each other, quietly, then one said my name, calling me Mister, still polite as Sunday morning. He tried the front door, rattled it gently against the latch, then walked sideways along the porch, a heavy pair of boots under the room I was sitting in. After more than a minute of silence I heard the back door window shatter. A moment later the door squeaked open and the boots were inside my house.

That was the meaning of forever, listening to those boots from room to room, slow as honey on a cold morning. Closet doors opened and closed. He went into the kitchen, seemed to stay there a full minute or two. When he crossed into the front hallway I got to my feet and came to the side of the bedroom door. He started up the stairwell and I was useless for any purpose but holding my breath and staring into that patch of invisible future that stands directly in front of a man's eyes. It is peculiar now to recollect that in a moment of such over-riding danger a man's imagination might rise like water to fill that place and show him a field of snow he last saw in his childhood, a frozen lake on a mountainside. In such a moment you might think nothing would move in a man except the trace of his fear, the taste of his own salt burning his tongue and the corners of his eyes, and to this day I remember the brief light of that winter memory, traveling to see my grandparents in a sleigh, horses steaming and trees in silver freeze. The road was disappeared, rivers snowed under and forests lost in the white. I could hear my visitor breathing as he reached the top step.

The smell of slept-in clothes and poor man's tobacco was strong on the landing. He stepped into the doorway and stopped.

He was not a large man and looked as if he might be quick

as he waited for his eyes to come around to the darkness in the bedroom. I pushed my shotgun's muzzle up against his neck.

He let out a small cry and stifled it. For a moment he didn't move, then he made to turn suddenly. I shifted the muzzle to just behind his head and let go one barrel into the empty hallway and my visitor fell flat.

The echo boomed around the house and I heard plaster and woodwork splinter and fall. My friend on the floor quivered face down; I smelled him as he soiled himself. He had been armed with a big Colt .44. The pistol was out in the middle of the bedroom floor. I straddled his body and lay the two barrels in at the base of his skull and I swear I have no idea what I said to him. In the years since I've imagined every manner of remark but the truth may be that I said nothing at all. I let him stand up — he thought he was mortally wounded — and walked him back downstairs with shit oozing in his trousers and the shotgun steadied between his shoulder blades. I directed him out the back door and onto the porch and his man was standing there and I know I told them both to start running. The partner was gone like a rabbit. I shoved my visitor with the shotgun and he fell off the porch into the mud and got up and ran like a cow into the field, grunting, slipping and whimpering. I lifted that old twelve-gauge and fired the second barrel into the stars.

■　■　■

I had my fill of heroism, the home-grown war survived, fighting to work on in a trade that would leave me breathless. As if, in the end, there was no way to win, no way to go home a satisfied man. Always something to hold you back, tear you down, work at killing you. So I take a fresh breath with all my mind on it, every bit of concentration, small rivers of air drawn along the edges of my nostrils, cool, a glide of vanishing light drawn into the darkness of my body. I do without the oxygen bottle as much as I can, as often as possible — a half-assed notion that the more I go without, the more I can do without. It does not happen that way, but a body hangs on to a vision of itself whole and intent on another good day just around the corner.

Out on an early morning drive. Winter, and the air cold enough to burn. The mines around Red Jacket are gone now, exhausted, folded, shut down. Phantom holes in the ground, mineral seeps and ruined tipples hanging off the black landslide out along south Route 16. Away in the distance you can smell the past moving around, the years riding alive. I can run down that thicket of a past always trying to lock it out or bring it up again, make it dream right in front of my eyes, hear my mother's voice again in the still afternoons of summer, back when summers were long as a year. *Raymond Dance, I will not have you talking that way.* And I'd call back *What way, Mama?* and she never answered that I can recall. That's the story of the past: what you remember best is what was not said. What I remember best turns like the silent pictures we watched in that Grange hall years ago, a world going on with nothing to deliver it forward but a double-bladed shadow and the salvation of time. Thinking of days gone before from the front seat of my truck — air bottle beside me like a friend coming along for the ride — and remembering is an act of farewell in itself, a goodbye to whatever belief in simplicity I might have had. God help us in the mouth of memory, on the last road home and free of any voice except our own.

I pass the big switching yard east of Red Jacket, a no man's land of grown-over track and drifters' fires. My Dodge pickup slips into the valley against a rush of flurried snow, out Main Street with that single row of houses hung on the ridgeline above town, everything waiting for the beginning of time or the end of the world. One or the other. Whichever comes first. The one stoplight in town moves through its changes out here in the cold, running the affairs of an empty street. I bring my truck into the parking lot at May's Diner and check my watch. Ten minutes past five. Alice says she simply cannot fathom, for the life of her, why I've taken to wandering around the countryside at the crack of dawn. I've told her why: to tell my story to myself, to get it straight in my mind, once and for all. I've explained that in order to do this, a man needs space and time and quiet. Well, she said, flat-voiced, I guess it's better than going out drinking at roadhouses till all hours of the night. I let it go at that.

Inside May's I take up a position at the counter with my oxygen bottle occupying the stool next door. May and I trade pleasantries before I ask for two eggs scrambled and a cup of black coffee. May nods and moves into the kitchen and I watch her go, knowing the picture that always comes back hardest is the night alone in that upstairs bedroom, waiting for all I knew to shoot a man dead next to the bed I shared with my wife, where our children were born. It had been my original intention never to tell Alice what had happened. After I sent the Baldwin boys off across the field I walked back upstairs and stopped in front of the piece of wall my shotgun had demolished. There was no way I could pretend that was an accident. I stood there in front of that big ragged hole thinking of Alice and the kids and I was overcome, sobbed with the shotgun cradled in my arms and my life seeming nothing more than a broken-down passage stained by chance and mishap, backroad losses and good blood in turn, all of us surrendered naked and never for what we know. As if there is a place in your life when the future is your best friend, the very thing that can save you. Whatever's possible will surely come to pass if you're patient, life will redeem itself and you are carried on with a young man's certainty. May brings the eggs and pours a cup of coffee and I thank her. Outside the frosted windows it's dawning and I can see the shape of the country that started it all. I take a sip of coffee and watch the mountains sail away toward Kentucky, and south.

JACKSON
STILLWELL

———

S HE WAS an old woman, walking with the sheriff in the orchard behind her house.

"We're gonna go on and declare him dead," the sheriff said.

She watched her feet move through fallen leaves.

"What was it, Edna?" the sheriff asked. "Epilepsy?"

She nodded. "Epilepsy," she said. "And not right in the head."

She stopped between two trees and the sheriff stopped beside her.

"That was the most of it," she went on. "Not right in the head. He couldn't have done what he did otherwise."

The sheriff squinted into the distance. "I reckon not."

"You know," Edna said, "this orchard used to be a beautiful place. Jackson would help me out here. He'd drag in apples in burlap sacks." She looked at the sheriff. "That's one thing that boy was good for. He could turn in a day's work."

"Yes ma'am." The sheriff fingered his hat brim.

"After a while," she said, "it just got to be too much for us. No matter how much we worked we couldn't keep up."

The sheriff took a breath. "The land'll do that to you. It can get away from a person."

Edna reached toward a tree, touching it. "Jackson told me he could taste apples when he chewed the skin of these trees." She studied the bark, considering.

The sheriff said he was sure he didn't know, and apologized for needing to leave so soon. He said he had another couple stops farther south.

"Well," she said. "I thank you for coming out."

The sheriff put on his hat, and told her it was no trouble at all. He hesitated a moment before he turned and walked back to his car and left her standing alone in her orchard in a breach of autumn light.

■　■　■

Edna Stillwell delivered her son Jackson into the world in the early summer of 1901. The doctor's solemn announcement confirming the boy's epilepsy and retardation would not come for five years after his birth, and Edna was fond of telling people the child had been born backward, *inside-out and into the hands of the Lord*, the last of her eight children and wrong from the first, haunted by the world like an animal too far from home. Her husband, twenty-one years her senior, died in his sleep two months after the birth. Her other children grown and gone, Jackson came up alone with his mother, a boy in constant awe staring into empty corners of the old house, standing astonished and bewildered at the windows during rainfall, passing days in his father's fallow barn, a private heaven of musk and bats' dung and the furtive lives of birds, his years falling in time. Alone in the barn he would collapse into seizure, eyes turned and lost in his head, his body locked in trance against a moving darkness. He would hear the voice of a woman and the pealing of bells or smell the approach of animals he had never seen, believing a celestial radiance flooded the barn's loft as he gathered his senses in the aftermath of each episode. He took crushing falls. There was a broken arm in an unconscious dive from the hay window, and his face carried the print of a pitchfork's tines, two perfect circles of scar side by side on his left cheek. The doctor rode out to the Stillwell place after the accidents, assessed the damage, comforted Jackson and Edna. On his last visit the doctor accepted a cup of tea, leaving Jackson on the front porch with a triangular bandage over a fractured collarbone.

In the kitchen the doctor stared into his cup. "That bone'll be all right in a few weeks if you can keep him quiet," he said. "You know I can't do anything about the rest."

"Well," Edna said. "It's no fault of yours."

"Still, a doctor wants to do what he can. At least say something of worth. I keep thinking the next time I come out they'll have a cure for epilepsy. A pill. Something Jack could drink once a day." He looked into his cup again, then finished the tea in a swallow.

Edna followed the doctor out and sat on the porch. It was midsummer of 1935 and she watched her son chipping weeds along a garden row, on his knees with a spade in his left hand.

His right arm swung gently in the sling. He showed no sign of pain. She sighed, sipped from her teacup. Lately, her ankles had been swelling at the end of a day. Her right eye was clouding over. Her hips ached on cold mornings. She did not ask herself what would become of her son when she was gone. Let the Lord provide.

She was seventy-eight years old.

■   ■   ■

Jackson Stillwell sat across from his mother in the plain kitchen as they finished a meal of garden beans and pone. He watched her, studying her chin, her rimless spectacles, considering his question. He had many questions, and more than once she had put him off, told him he could not hope to understand. He believed his questions might reveal the face of a secret world, an open road into what everybody else seemed to have, and he asked his mother about clouds and rivers, about time and light and rain, where they came from and why. He was fascinated by dreams and Edna struggled with versions of her own truth. *Pictures and voices that come to you while you're sleeping. The visions you receive, that travel through your mind.* Jackson Stillwell was convinced his personal redemption would come in the form of a dream and he asked his mother, "Mama, what was the first dream you ever had?"

He had no memory of dreaming. He believed he had never dreamed, that when he fell asleep he simply vanished.

Edna looked at her son, then at the kitchen's one window. "God, boy," she said. "The first dream I ever had. I don't know as I could truthfully say."

Jackson grinned, waited for her story.

She looked down at her plate. "I know I would dream from the stories my daddy told me," she said. "He'd tell a ghost story and I'd dream about it that night, wake up all shivery, have to go in and sleep with him and Mama. He'd tell a funny story, my brothers'd say I was laughing in my sleep."

She turned again to the window. "Now there's a thing," she went on. "Laughing in your sleep. 'Course I don't know that's true. Not with my brothers to tell it. But my very first dream? If I ever did know, I surely don't know now."

Jackson gazed at her, weighing what he had heard. Then he said, "Mama, I been thinking about Ramona. Wishing she'd come back."

Edna Stillwell got up from the table and passed through the back door to the pump in the yard. A mongrel was limp in the weathered-out porch shade, watching her, and when she looked at the three-room house she knew her son was inside, alone at the kitchen table, staring at the open doorway she had moved through. She still called him *boy*, the man with two days' growth of beard who asked about her dreams.

■　■　■

Jackson sailed the south meadow to the east of his mother's house, checking his traps, kicking a yellow down out of the wild alfalfa and sweet clover. He came on a trap full of rabbit, the animal dead at least a day, pulled the lock and drew out the rigid corpse. With the rabbit against a thatch of mustard grass he stretched a front paw clear of the body, cleaved the foot away in one fall of his hatchet and put the paw in the soft cloth bag his mother had made for him. Standing and walking he felt the sun move in the sky and for a moment he thought he heard someone call his name, a woman's voice. He stopped in the middle of the broad meadow, listening for the bells he heard when he was about to have what his mother always called a spell, bells blowing out of the air. He looked up at the glaze of clouds. *Sit down boy*, his mother had told him, *sit down when you feel a spell coming on*, and he told her *Sometimes Mama I'm so weak I can't do nothing, I just want it to come and take me over and be done with it*, as if a storm could move up and over the horizon so suddenly he was riveted by the black clouds climbing into the air. Jackson Stillwell stood in his rabbit-trap meadow in a spill of summer as his eyes rolled away from the light, arms pushing out of the seizure and reaching as he fell like a tree coming down, arms and legs rigid in convulsion, his quivering body lifting a feathered mist of pollen.

■　■　■

From where he fell he looked into the sky while his eyes came back to focus and his memory returned in pieces. He watched for pictures and signs in the shapes of the clouds. He sang quietly to himself. He thought of Ramona; the meadow had been a favorite place to play when they were children. For years Ramona's aunt visited Jackson's mother, and Ramona came with her, bringing gifts from town: cut flowers that smelled of jasmine and water, persimmons with their wet bitterness on Jackson's chin, a ball and jacks. On one visit she brought postcards. From France, Ramona told him. Images of Brittany countryside with peasants bending in wheat, harlequins dancing in front of a fountain, two ladies in a garden with parasols. Ramona told stories to accompany each scene and Jackson took them for true.

They chased across pasture and into forest, hide and seek, Ramona laughing and running ahead under a spackled fall of light in the elder and boxwood and black cherry, pounding ankle-deep across creeks, rolling slopes until the sky swam.

As Ramona grew older her aunt made more visits alone, telling Jackson that Ramona was becoming a young lady, with other things to do, other people to see. Jackson was polite. He wanted to conceal his fear. He never knew how or why he was changing and saw Ramona Snow on his few town trips and felt her distance growing even as she greeted him, smiling, kissing him on the cheek.

■   ■   ■

At times, and always at night from his bed, Jackson Stillwell heard music. He was convinced he heard music, and left his bed to walk from the house into the night in his long underwear and bare feet. Moonlight edged the crowns of maples as he searched for what he had heard, as if he could walk out on the road and turn one way or another and find a musician along the roadside with an instrument on one knee, a dulcimer or a banjo, sitting and playing. The music was a part of the night, inside the night, and Jackson could not be sure but he tried to listen, he bit his lower lip working hard to listen.

There were nights he walked over two miles from the house, walking barefoot until he knew how late it was and how alone he was and that he no longer heard the music. He heard what he knew was there: a slow wind on the move across alfalfa fields and corn rows, crickets, frogs now and again from the direction of water. He tried to remember the music as he walked back to his mother's house, tried to recollect the chain of melody a man could climb if he was listening right. On the night in July when he heard the music again he got out of bed, pulled on his trousers and left the house, turning south at the gate and walking along the dirt lane. He followed the music as far as he could, as far as it took him along the road, along the line of creek that pulled in from the west, and off, toward the river. He was taking the music to Ramona. He would remember it and take it to her and sing it to her, standing beside her bed. He would take his gift to Ramona and they would walk together along the road and into the forest and he would have her back again.

The moon was mid-sky, nearly full, bright and cold and clean, and he walked the four miles to the north edge of town, to the Snow house.

As he opened the gate the family dog stood on the porch and barked once, jumped down and came toward him through the grass. Jackson waited, knelt and stroked the animal when it reached him, leaving it contented on its side as he moved in against the back wall of the house, stepping carefully below the windows. The window he remembered as Ramona's was open, a white curtain drifting. He pulled himself up and over the sill until he sat in the window frame, and dropped quietly inside the room.

The curtain blew across the sill and flattened against his back, lifted away again to billow and fill the window.

When he was a boy he had sat on the floor of this same bedroom with one of Ramona's first powder puffs, batting it over the hardwood. He tried to put it in his mouth and Ramona pulled it away, laughing: *No, silly, you can't eat it.* The room smelled as it had then, of varnished spruce and clean bedding and body powder.

He watched the woman he knew must be Ramona, her hair dark and fanned over the pillow as he let his own breath slip into time with the rise and fall of her body, wondering if she was dreaming. She was on her side and Jackson stared, thinking that if he looked long enough he would see what she was dreaming, he would have a vision of the inside of her night and it would become his own, second sight, the thing he would carry away. He could tell his mother he knew what a dream looked like. That he had one of his own.

She moved in her sleep, groaning softly; from somewhere in the house Jackson heard a sound. He could not be sure: the whisper of a curtain parted in front of an open window. A body coming out of bed. A match being struck or a foot across a floorboard, and Jackson remembered Ramona's father. He had seen him once, big man washing coal dust from a huge neck and shoulders and chest, splashing creek water from a tub on the porch, angry red moustache, muscles alive inside his arms, and Jackson dived through the open window, back to the grass and breaking for the fence and the pasture beyond, sure he had heard a sound and it would be Ramona's father filling the doorway of her bedroom, and the dog barked and chased to the fence but Jackson was over, running up the long hill behind the house until his lungs and ribs and legs burned with the effort. A hundred yards out he stopped, panting, turned to look back. The house sat alone and quiet, innocent, small from where he stood. Around him, everywhere, the grass moved like water.

■　　■　　■

When Jackson heard the music again it was early September and he moved barefoot through the pastures, toward the village where lights flickered across the cover of darkness as if they lived inside his head. He walked and thought *Look at me*, tip of his tongue showing between his lips in concentration.

The Snow house rose out of the night: wing porch, shutters, roof peak. Jackson opened the gate, moved through and closed it behind him and the dog was there, nuzzling at his leg, lying at his feet.

Wading grass to the back of the house, Jackson saw Ramona's window still open to the cooler nights and he pulled up on the frame, got his feet through and curled his body in and settled on the floor with his hands braced against the sill and the woman in the bed sat up. There was a moment before she whispered *Who's there?*

Jackson held his breath, staring at her, unable to speak.

She pulled the sheet up to cover herself, leaning forward looking at him, at his shape.

"Mr. Stillwell?" She got out of bed. The dread in her whisper was gone. She turned her back and put on a robe. He let his breath go, began to breathe again.

Standing in front of him she said, "What are you doing here?" Her voice was soft, and seemed to move over his face like cool air. As if he were hearing her with his skin.

"This is very wrong, Mr. Stillwell. You should know that."

He felt as if his face might slide away. His mouth was moving; he was trying to speak.

"You," he said. "You're not Ramona."

"No," she said. "Ramona's married and gone. A long time gone, nearly eight years."

"You're not Ramona," Jackson said again.

"I'm her younger sister," the woman said. "Becky. You remember me."

Jackson started to speak, and stopped. His mouth was dry. "I came to see Ramona," he said.

"Well," Becky Snow said, gently, speaking to a child. "It's like I told you. She's not here. She doesn't live here anymore."

Jackson studied the room, searching. "I thought this was Ramona's room."

"It was, years ago. Mr. Stillwell? Do you know what time it is?"

Jackson looked at her in wonderment, as if she spoke a foreign language he should understand, but did not.

"Mr. Stillwell? You're going to have to leave now." From deeper in the house a man's voice called her name; she turned to the door and said, "It's all right, Daddy."

Jackson's head made two involuntary beats to the right, a spasm riding down his neck. "I wanted to watch her sleep," he said softly. The muscles in his chest began to drum.

Becky said, "It's proper to visit people during the day. You know that. I don't need to tell you that."

"I wanted to watch her sleep," he said again. "I just wanted to stand here. I would never hurt her."

They looked at each other and Jackson did not speak, hearing the bells. He heard them from under the hills, beyond the horizon. Two heavenly notes ringing over and over, filling the room, coming to eat what little light there was, a spirit he could see at a distance, walking toward him on the air. He could smell a fire, ashes blowing into the house.

Becky said, "I know you only came to see Ramona."

"I only came to see her," he said. His head wobbled against his will.

"It's very sweet of you. I'll tell Ramona you're wanting to visit. But you have to go now."

Jackson saw smoke seeping into the room, pluming from under the bed and he was gone, possessed and flailing, falling backward through the window to rip away the curtain. Beneath the window on his back, convulsing delirious in the bluegrass and chewing away the end of his tongue as the sky rolled and fell open and his mouth filled with blood. Rebecca Snow shouted for her father.

■　　■　　■

Jackson Stillwell wandered, living on plantain and creek water in parts of the high forest only the Shawnee had seen before him. He had been gone from home for days and imagined himself on horseback, the horse underneath him with the same smoking nostrils and blood-red eyes he had seen in picture books. They climbed together into mist and black water, shapes of wings in silhouette above them. He saw the shadow of his windswept hair gliding the ground and the shadow of Ramona in the saddle behind him, holding him around the waist. Ramona as he had always wanted her, in a place they could live forever, singing the hymns they learned in church as children. Jackson sang and listened to the music come back to him out of the wind and did not know he was lost, believing his mother's house would rise behind every ridge as he walked on obsessed with what he thought were the voices of angels. On the fifth day out he found a young rabbit cowering in a cave, killed it with a stone and ate the meat raw.

Sleeping in leaves, he woke with spiders on his eyelids. Morning birds called in the reaches of the trees.

■   ■   ■

There were those prepared to defer to Christ when Jackson turned up missing, those who argued for a divine salvation in the wilderness. The search went on for more than a week.

The sheriff organized a posse with six men and hunting dogs. They plotted out the countryside, and their campfires could be seen from town on the ridges to the east, north, northwest, finally south along the river. They found no trace of Jackson Stillwell and came home on mud-spattered horses, riding into town in a downpour, the weary dogs stringing behind.

The days moved toward autumn and it was finally Edna alone in the mountains, stopping the few travelers she saw to ask about her lost son, passing the dark hours in half-sleep under the palisades and scree. Night rooted in the wind driving across the canyons' faces, the gone picture of time in an old woman's one good eye. At a summit after a pointless climb she sat down exhausted, knowing he was gone and his disappearance would fade to the quiet turn of mind in the listener hearing the story years away. She thought of the morning in the kitchen he had asked about her first dream. That afternoon he had come home from his traps and sat on the step, pulled out the drawstring on the pouch she had made for him and emptied rabbits' feet onto the porch, eight paws scattered across the planks. He had looked up at her, his face sweat-rimmed, needing a shave, and he said *I gathered these for you, Mama. They will bring you good fortune forever.*

She had nodded and smiled and thanked him.

Jack, she had said, *a touch of good fortune is surely what every woman needs.*

ROCK OF
AGES

At times the old man is talking alone, half blind as time in the old-woman hills, sleepwalking. Luther sees him scraping around the cabin on the moon's light, denim trousers scratching, old man mumbling, old man pissing against the wall in his sleep, and Luther gets out of bed and goes to him: *Come on Daddy, you're dreaming, let's go back to bed.* Old man growling, rumbling as he pushes his son away, and Luther says *Daddy, you're asleep, you don't know what you're doing.* The old man opens his eyes, looking at Luther as if he cannot recognize him, saying *Let me tell you the story of how your little brother come into this world.*

Daddy, I know that story.

You don't. You don't know the half of it.

You told me a lotta times Luther says as he leads his father back to bed, old man's bare feet scratching wood planks, one trouser leg wet with urine to the knee, old man murmuring, whispering, lost in his night.

■   ■   ■

The story of Luther's brother's birth is one of the old man's favorites, his private darkness rivering the night and whispering color into the flat corners of a hot room. *Your brother,* he rasps, voice a perfect ember, *was born with seven fingers on each hand.* He pauses, his one working eye in lantern beam, before he goes on. *And he has two hearts,* old man tapping his chest with a broad dirty finger, *one on the left and one on the right.* He leans back, wheezing a philosophical sigh. *He was born that way,* the old man says, gazing down at the floor, blinking over a black socket, his glass eye and a lily together in a bowl of water on the table beside him, wavering in fireplace shadow.

Luther watches the way his brother can look all day at nothing at all, that long-summer's-day face as he talks to his brother, sitting beside him on the front porch swing telling about the places he imagines he will go and things he will do when he gets there as if a lifetime stretches away from everything he can see. He tells his brother stories about animals that speak and it seems at times his brother listens, a slight smile turning at what might have been the right moment in the story, and Luther can never be sure.

■ ■ ■

The old man comes home drunk. He has his share of trouble with the three front steps, porch yawning in front of him like a dry riverbed, bottle banging against the door frame as he tries to get into the house. The old man carefully places the bottle in the center of the table with a trace of ceremony and collapses into a chair saying *A touch of rain in the air, yes indeed.* Luther waits; the old man looks around the room as if something is missing but he cannot say what. *Probably rain by midnight,* the old man says. Luther nods. From the sofa Luther's brother howls, long restless blade of a wail, and when the sound dies away the old man says *There he goes again. Calling the coyotes.* Nearly every night there is the howling and Luther feels hopeless and confused as if nothing is right in the world, nothing can ever be right. The old man takes a swallow of bourbon, replacing the bottle at its position in the middle of the table, leans back looking at the boy on the sofa who gazes into the past or the future. *Now ain't that the ass end of chance*, the old man says. *My woman died bringing that boy into this world. It's a rare day goes by I don't ask myself where the justice is in that.* The old man looks at Luther. *Don't you miss your mama, boy? Because we traded your sweet mama for that little man over there on the couch. Know that?* Luther draws a long breath, looking away; the old man takes another drink. Luther's brother waves his head from one wall to another, slowly, his eyes filled with a prodigal light.

■　　■　　■

Luther's brother fevered, coughing, his skin the color of a summer sky. The cough rides up from the center of his chest, wet and malicious; he heaves from his place on the sofa, convulsions of bad air. When the coughing subsides he looks toward Luther and his face carries the same emptiness it always has. The old man is nowhere to be found.

Luther's brother wheezes, rocks forward with the effort of breathing. Luther watches a moment before he gets up and pulls the trunk from under the old man's bed, takes out a coat and a blanket, puts them both on the sofa. *Now you just rest easy*, Luther says. *I'll be back.*

As if that boy can go anywhere Luther thinks as he runs downslope to the barn. In half-light he steps to the last stall, kicking clear of straw, hearing the skitter of mice, and the wagon is where he left it, spotted by bird dung, wood-slat rails weathered from Christmas-morning red to a watery rose. The wagon Luther had pulled everywhere filled with stones, with mud, carting piglets and lambs around the barnyard. Begging the old man to pull him in the wagon, *Just one more ride*, the old man lifting him into the cart, *Mind yourself boy, hold on tight*, wooden wheels bumping over rock outcrop and sun-dried manure, old man laughing as the goat trotted behind the wagon in weak chase and Luther's mother wiped her hands on her apron, watching from the porch with that generous smile opening in her face. *Like that, do ya?* the old man would call out, trying to move the wagon faster, make the turns sharper, Luther holding on to the rails as the barnyard whirled. In the days before his brother came, before his mother was gone and the old man went bitter.

Luther carries the wagon across the barnyard to the base of the porch steps. Inside the house his brother is coughing, spittle foam at the corners of his mouth and bestial gaze searching the air. *Sit tight there, little buddy*, Luther says, *I'm gonna get you out of here. I'm gonna get you some help*.

Luther lines the wagon bed with the blanket and goes back into the cabin and wraps his brother in the coat. *Come on now, little man.* Luther carries him to the wagon and props the trembling skull against a rail, saying *Now you just don't worry, I'm gonna find the doctor.* Luther takes the wagon downgrade and into the forest at the crest of the hill, carrying where he has to, grunting over gullies and washouts, over fallen trees, and halfway down the mountainside reaches the horse trail that will fall to the Clarksburg Road.

■　■　■

Luther often tried to look into his brother's eyes, eyes filled with snow and Luther would be reminded of animals, the innocence of small creatures surprised at the edge of a clearing very early in the morning. The mute surprise of a deer who had been lost in the rightful world of the forest and wandered too easily into a broken fall of sunlight. Luther believed his brother carried the same innocence, invisible unless the light moved across his face in an accidental pattern and Luther saw the spirit abandoned there, inside the veined skull waving like grasses on the bottom of a river.

The doctor who delivered Luther's brother into the world and pronounced his mother dead in the same hour had claimed the infant would not see six months, and Luther's brother had lived the five years since in the corner of the chartreuse sofa without a day going by that was different from the day that went before it or came after it. Luther washed his brother's diapers in a tub beside the house, winter and summer, knocking the smeared waste into a hole he had dug at the brow of the hill and bringing the diapers back to the fire-heated water, pushing them under the steam with a sycamore stick, lathering the yellowed muslin with a bar of lye soap, on a washboard.

■　■　■

Luther rattles the wagon along the edge of the Clarksburg Road, his body aching and mountains soaring away from the lip of the road in mist. Every few moments he looks back at his brother's head wobbling forward and a strand of glistening spittle swaying at his chin. The wagon bounces and creaks and Luther does not see the horseman approach.

Ho, boy, the horseman says, reining in; Luther is startled, suddenly frightened. He stops, holding the wagon tongue in two hands behind his back. The horseman brings his animal forward two paces and leans in the saddle to look at Luther and then at Luther's brother.

Hard day for a boy to be out, the man on the horse says, looking up at the air. *Gonna rain any time.*

Luther nods, says *I got to get my brother here to the doctor. He's terrible sick.*

The horseman studies Luther's brother a moment, then he says *You're Luther Tanner?*

Yes sir.

You're taking your brother into town? You come all the way down from your place by yourself?

Yes sir.

With that wagon?

Yes sir.

Where's your daddy?

Luther hesitates. The horseman watches him, and Luther finally says *I don't know.*

The horseman sighs and dismounts and Luther sees the butt of a holstered Colt .44. The horseman identifies himself as Deputy Sheriff Roy John and says that he remembers Luther but it's been years and Luther may not recall. He says he has even been up to the Tanner place for Sunday dinner once, back when Mrs. Tanner was alive. He kneels beside the wagon, looking in at Luther's brother, saying *Your mother was a fine woman.* The sheriff studies the child in the wagon, touching the white underside of one wrist with two fingertips. He lifts the child's face: snow-blue eyes swim in a blind drift, toward the sky. Roy John pulls open the coat Luther wrapped his brother in and feels inside, against the child's chest, and then he sighs again and stands and says *Luther, you did everything you could do.*

■ ■ ■

Luther and the old man carry the child's body in a cherrywood box to a grave under a maple down the hill from the house, preacher walking behind reading aloud from the Bible. Rainfall moves on an edge of heat, blowing through the maple's crown. The old man shovels the shallow ditch closed and they walk slowly back to the house in a line, uphill with the preacher leading and the old man behind Luther in a dirty black suit with a collarless white shirt buttoned to his neck. The old man unslings the concertina he carries and pumps a breath across its reeds as he walks; it groans over an exhausted chord and he plays "Rock of Ages," dry and torn on the summer wind. The song ends as they reach the house, and Luther lets the two men go inside as he lingers on the porch looking down the August meadow, a haze of ochre and lilac. When he hears the drone of the preacher in practiced consolation he goes over the banister, drops to meadowgrass, breaking a run at the brushline with the first fall of rain.

It is a downpour in the forest and he runs, flushing squirrels and jackrabbits, wishing he could go faster, with a horse. Or that he could fly, the sun behind clouds a trapped light he would ride as far as he could into the rain, legs burning like guns. Luther had sat with his brother on the porch during rainfall, his brother listening to the roar and tilting his head against the sound, one ear and then the other. His eyes were fixed and for once in focus, as if he could see water in its own house, could see where it came from and where it was going. Luther would talk to his brother then as if they were boys waiting to go after the frogs that would be everywhere in the rain's wake, and he felt a contentment in those moments, loving the pale of mist and cold air in the middle of a mountain summer, as if the rain would fade and the sky would clear and he and his brother would walk away together.

Coming out of the forest Luther stops at the treeline and looks across the meadow to his brother's grave under the tree that is swirling, whipped and bowed by the storm. Luther stands, hair matted, water in rivulets around his nose and off his chin, watching the little mound of earth that covers his brother's box slide into mud.

■ ■ ■

The old man leaves the house with a bottle. Luther on his back in bed, alone in the cabin for the first time in his life, wonders if the old man is celebrating at the roadhouse down the mountain, telling everybody he is free at last of the little man who killed his wife these five years ago and stayed on to do nothing but shit his pants and bay at the moon like some kind of hopeless animal every single night. There is the sound of a train in the distance. Birds flutter in the cabin's eaves. Luther stares at the stained plank ceiling, tracing islands and stars in the aging pine, nightfall over another country. When he finally falls asleep he dreams his hair is turning to wood, soaked and black like old trees cut adrift in a flood, and a shower of voices fights the wind, cascading from some empty heaven, blown open and raining into his sleep.

THE
WARS
OF
HEAVEN

LISTEN. Hear me talking to you. Rockwell Lee Junior remembering the glow in your kitchen, Mama, the light that was a mix of gold and blue on a winter's night and the way our talk drifted around like big slow birds in the warm air and Oh what I wouldn't give for one more day in the sweetness of what I didn't know back when, the days before, when I was just a grinning boy in a dirty white shirt, an innocent yes indeed. Or the afternoons sitting at your kitchen table when you'd make me a mug of your coffee, Mama, and sweeten it with clover honey and color it with goat's milk. Always liked your coffee, you know that I did, even when I was a kid I'd ask you for a taste and you'd let me sip from your cup and Daddy grinning at me from across the table. I remember the little circle of heat that would come up from your cup, touch my lips, and what I wouldn't have given for a cup of your coffee, trapped as I was in that icehouse of a sky full of snow where any direction I looked and as far as I could see it was white, whiteness in the trees, humped up against the mountains, whiteness. At least the wind had died down, that was the morning of St. Valentine's Day, at least I could say that because that's what kills you, that's what steals the air out of your lungs, steals the light straight out of your eyes, if anything can do that it's the wind in winter across a field of snow bearing down on you like a ghost train out of nowhere. Early that morning the wind passed off to the north, I could nearly see it go, so God was merciful and I thanked God for that. I dropped to my knees taking care to keep my rifle butt-down and upright leaning against my left shoulder, and I prayed. Thank you Jesus. No wind today. No wind to freeze what life I got left, to steal the light out of my eyes. Thank you Jesus. One more day of life. And Mama, you might ask how it was the condemned man still prayed to his God in the wilderness, you'll say What could I have to say to God and Jesus out there on the run Where could I be going that was any salvation at all after what I done. Maybe this is all I really wanted, a chance at rectitude, restitution by myself and alone and in a place of my own choosing. A simple place where what dreams I might still have harbored could die a tranquil death, lonely as time itself and peaceful as light. And you know the sheriff's posse caught up to me here at Judson Church so there may be a justice in this, an understanding. You know you always said that dreams were made of water and human desire, that dreams went no mortal place at all, they were only man's way to confuse himself and convince himself that a fire was lit at the heart of things. You always said it was nothing but cinder and ashes and now I don't know, the way I walked out there in that whole world of snow with that posse surely on my trail, I don't know, I swear I can't be sure. When I shot that girl you know I saw her fall down right there on her daddy's porch, fall down like a puppet whose strings got cut and I swear I saw the life drawing out of her like light coming out of a window at night. And I was not the man you knew. In that instant I was not the man you ever knew. I was that skeleton engineer on the phantom locomotive in that scare-story you told when I was a kid, I was just one headlong scream into oblivion I swear. At the moment she fell down like an empty sack and I knew what I had done I was lost as I am right now up here in the hills in the snow. Now that it's all too late I think you were wrong, Mama, I think that there is a light down somewhere in the center of things and that if a man knew that for a solid fact he could go down to that place and warm his hands on a cold night. Because how could I be so desperate and finished and on the run and see everything so beautiful and transfixing and everlasting, everywhere I turned was like looking forever, like a picture up on somebody's wall so I had to stop and stand and look into the world for the first and last time, wondering why I never saw it before.

When I got to Judson Church there was enough wood to light a fire and I hung my coat and warmed myself over that stove and thanked the Lord there was no moon that night, no moonlight to let any sheriff's posse see my smoke. No moonlight to show my footprints walking across the snowfield and right up to the church steps. I'd been on the move at night, hiding in tumble-down houses all day with my rifle up and ready and afraid to sleep, and I had my time to think, reflect on things, see where it had all gone bad, and Mama, you know I think it was losing Daddy that did it to us, both of us. It was losing Daddy that took the life out of you, took your own life away from you, that made you so hard and tired and unforgiving. That let your own bitterness rail against you inside like a snow-wind of the very heart and soul I swear, that made you turn away in your loss and violent mind. Mama, I think you died on that old covered bridge with Daddy, I swear I think you did. Daddy was the true anchor, he was the root our lives were growing from when he died only we didn't know it, we were innocents, the two of us. So you claim you know Daddy's killer, that you'd know the face of the devil if you looked straight into that face, and maybe so. But I don't know. All we know is Daddy's body was found on that bridge with his watch and money gone, that's all we really know, and it could have been anybody, it could have been a neighbor or a stranger and we'll never know and that's a fact.

So it's a terrible strange thing that I came to be the very one that killed Daddy for a pittance in the cover of darkness. For we are all of one bad wind, you know that, Mama, all of us robbers and murderers are one evil man split down into a hundred wild boys, all doing the cruel bidding of some kind of master within. I had heard that before and now I know it to be true but I never once thought about it, what was happening to me, I never once saw it all coming as I should. I could have turned back a hundred times but I didn't, I was like a man on a spooked horse, riding straight into the eyes of a fire and just hanging on for dear life.

You could say it was friends or circumstance or some of both but I can feel now it was simply Daddy going out the way he did, lost the way he was in some terrible whirlpool of time and I swear I was nothing but a useless boy hanging on a spike thrown this way and that, born under a bad sign, condemned to howl at the moon, to preach to the wind, and I drifted like a rotting boat cut loose on floodwaters after a hard rain, beating from one tree to another until I was out in the main current and running. And that's the way it goes, out there in the deep water with some other power under you and driving you, keeping you whole until finally you hit the rapids and go over the falls.

That's how I came to be in on the robbery of Strother's Store over in the mining camp. The other boys wanted to do it, claimed old Strother kept a mint under the floor behind the cashbox, and I said Well okay. When we got over there I felt no fear, I still cannot explain how I walked right up on the porch and butted my rifle right through the plate glass and opened the door and walked inside like it was my store and not Strother's, but let me tell you it inspired a measure of confidence in those boys that went inside behind me, yes indeed. And you know the strange thing is, I walked into that store holding my rifle up like I was looking to shoot something, walked in and straight back past them tables all laid up with can-goods and linens and bottled water, right back to the rear wall where Strother had all his bridles and reins hung up, and I turned around to face front, leaned against the wall and just stood there. I didn't want a goddamned thing. I didn't care about money, or the things worth stealing in that store. I felt then as I did ever since. I felt mad with temper, and like I could just keep it under my skin if nobody pushed at me. And so goddamned afraid. Afraid of what I've never been truly sure, but I know if the sheriff walked into the middle of that robbery or any other one and shot us all down I wouldn't have much cared, that's the kind of feeling I'm speaking of. And I felt that way until the day I hit Judson Church and looked back on what had gone before, and knew I had to wait in that little house of the Lord, wait there for my redemption in whatever form it was coming and at least I was in a sanctified place.

So I just stood there in Strother's Store while the boys

whooped it up and made a mess of the place, and Bob Hanks came back to me, said Rocky what's the matter? And I said I'm just fine, Bob. You just go on and do what you came to do, that's all. And Bob looked at me strange a moment but went on back to work, and when the boys was still and quiet and standing in the doorway with their bags full up I walked over to where they stood and past them and out the door. I stepped down to the road and got in behind the wheel of your truck, Mama, started it up. The boys all filed down and got in, climbed onto the bed, and nobody said a word to me.

They had found old Strother's money pile and split it five ways. Three thousand dollars and change. Everything Strother had in the world and Bob Hanks came over to me with six one-hundred-dollar bills saying This here's your share Rock. And I said Thank you kindly and Bob drew on the whiskey bottle he'd been carrying around and grinned at me. Well sir, he said, you're quite welcome.

And you know, Mama, it was all my plans after that, the branch bank over in Federalsville, the general store out to Middle River, right down to the night I shot Betty Shadwell dead on her daddy's front porch and knew I had become the man who speaks to you now in the sure voice of death, dead in the ice, you might even say in the frozen waste of time. Out here in the snow it is surely the end of the world. I could hear the sound of my breath setting up against the air like a rasp: the end of the world I swear.

Outside the church it was going to sunset, the day's light drawing down to that twilight filled with fire-color that burns on the snow before it proceeds to die right into the night. I stirred the wood on the grate and was thankful for that bit of stove heat, wrapped my coat around me and tried to lay down on a pew and saw it wasn't going to work. So I went on and laid down on the floor up against the back wall of the church with a Philadelphia hymnal under my head and the Winchester right there in easy reach. But sleep wasn't about to come. No ma'am. I just lay there, listening to the mice scrap and itch around the floorboards, thieves like me, looking for what isn't there, for what will never be there, and you know how your mind goes into a kind of trance when you're too tired to sleep, how you think crazy things, think the moon moves faster than it does? I lay there on the floor of Judson Church and lived in that half-a-dream, and I saw your face, Mama, and I saw Daddy's, and I saw Rita Clair's face too, it was Rita as I saw her the last time up on the hill over town, sitting on a blanket with that man's workshirt on over nothing, her dress and underwear laid to one side on the grass. We made love up there on that hill, squatting down on that old blanket and moving together and the bees moaning around us and crickets working, every now and again a hot breeze come to rustle in our hair. I had my hands up under that shirt, all over her like I wanted to be more than just inside her, I wanted to melt into her. As if I could just disappear and become part of that one moment, forever, lost in it, outside of this voice that speaks to you now. I raised my face to the sky and the sky was blue as I had never seen and there were clouds as white and soft and eternal-looking as you can imagine and I swear it was as if me and Rita were being raised together into that sky, lifted up, me holding Rita and her in my lap, the both of us panting and wheezing and crying out. We went up in the air floating right out over the brow of that hill, then we started to come down like we were stones settling to the bottom of a slow river, coming down through green light and silence, our ears filled up, our eyes covered over and I thought then, That's right, we're just like rocks thrown into a river. You don't know where you come from or where you're gone, you just get picked up and thrown. But you can have one little moment, yes sir, you can have Rita Clair's sweet fine body on a hill in the middle of a hot summer so as to have a glimpse of what might have been, like looking through a little crack into the future or the past and not knowing which way you're looking, but seeing it all filled up with light and the smell of honey. I laid there, Mama, remembering everything I tell you now, Daddy going the way he did, you turning away from me in your grief, having that little taste of Rita Clair, that little glimpse of heaven and knowing I wasn't fit to have no more than that, and the way I went to stealing and could hate myself so bad and still be so calm, standing at the window of the church and seeing the sheriff and his deputies out there at the treeline like I knew they would be, just shapes out there in those long coats and big hats and the straight black lines of their rifle barrels up against the snow.

There was a thin light seeping into the church, that watery first light you get on a winter dawn. I stood up and shook out of my coat and went to the window and there they were, standing out there looking at my trace across the snowfield, the way it ended right at the church steps.

I turned away from the window, sat down in a pew. They wouldn't just walk up to the door and knock. No sir. Not with a man like me inside. Sheriff'd try to get me to come out peaceable, lay down my gun, throw it out in the snow. But he'd be prepared to shoot me.

I got my rifle and went to the window on the other side of the church, unlocked it and slid it up. The stained-glass face of Jesus rose up in front of me and then I saw the snow stretching down to Rucker's Creek and I leaned out and propped my piece against the outside wall of the church, let myself out and down to the snow, waited. I heard nothing. I knew they wouldn't come across the pasture, not with the risk of me being inside the church. They'd be fanning out just inside the treeline, trying to surround me. I started for the trees thinking I could at least get into the woods myself. The snow was frozen over, a crust my boots dropped through an inch, and I saw they'd track me anywhere I went but I had to go, there was nothing else to do. I was halfway to the treeline when I heard my name called out, hollow, booming around in the air. I turned and it was Stewart McCarty standing under the stained-glass window I'd left out of with his scattergun trained down on me. *Mr. Lee*, he called out, *just stand where you are real still and put down your rifle.* I could see the smoke of his breath. I raised my Winchester and fired, hit Stewart somewhere above the waist and he grunted, slammed back against the church and slid a red streak down the wall, flopping around in the snow. I turned and ran for the trees.

I could hear the sound of the creek and a man I thought looked like Roy John stepped around in some birches up to my right, and then I knew it was him when he yelled to me *Rockwell Lee, give yourself up now. No use in running no more.*

I turned to the direction of his voice. New snow started to fall. His shape moved back and forth in the trees. *Roy*, I called out. *Roy, help me. What happened, it was an accident.*

Roy John came into full view, aiming his rifle at me. I thought I saw movement behind him. Snow filled the air.

Roy, I said. *Roy, you know me. You know my mama.*

I know what you done, Rock. You're gonna have to come home with us.

The peculiar thing is that I had no intention of killing anyone at the Shadwell place, there or any other place, we just meant to get on out of there with the silver because Bob Hanks knew where the old man kept it in the house. If the old man hadn't come out of the house firing his pistol. I just meant to let go a warning shot, blow out a front window, I swear I didn't even see Betty there on the porch, what was she doing there anyway? You answer me that. I didn't even see her till she fell. Rockwell Lee Junior may have been a robber but he was no murderer. That was a pure accident. It was never meant to be. No sir. So when I lifted my rifle with the intent to throw it down and give myself up and tell my story, Roy John blew off my left shoulder.

The force of it shoved me back and I stumbled, and I had the strangest feeling of surprise but I stayed on my feet and kept hold of my gun. Blood and bone and muscle had sprayed out over the snow like a mist, I could look right down into the hole in my coat where my shoulder had been, an awful burning and the falling snow melting in the wound, steam wisping up out of the hole and my shoulder looking that way got me angry, mad with temper all over again and that terrible fear and I raised my Winchester over my head with my right arm yelling *Goddamn you, Roy, look what you done.*

The second shot was a shotgun, catching me square in the chest, I went off the ground, legs kicking and the force of that shot knocking my right boot off. Damn if I was going to let them take me laying on the ground, I got up again and don't you know I was an awful mess, I looked like the mouth of hell, blood everywhere and my coat hanging on me in rags.

I swayed there in the falling snow. My breath was hard to come by, I could hear air sucking right in through the holes in my chest and the whole lot of them come out of the trees then, the sheriff, Roy John, the rest of the deputies just coming up around me and looking at me and I could see it was Stewart McCarty who fired the shotgun round. He was back on his feet under that Jesus window and at first I thought I had been shot by a ghost but then I knew I had only wounded him. My eyesight began to go on me then, frayed around the edges in all that whiteness and air filled with snow like an old sheet hung out to dry and coming apart in a heavy wind. Roy John walked up to me and took off his long coat and put it around me. The sheriff came up behind Roy to handcuff my wrists together and standing there half-dead for sure I heard the sound of bells, out in the distance of that snowy air, out in some reach of that wild snowy air there was the slow music of bells and I looked out to the hills and clouds trying to see where that music came from and why it was coming to me. Roy John looked at me and said *What is it, Rock?*

And I said *Roy, don't you hear 'em? Like church bells.* I raised the handcuffs, my hands clasped together in a fist pointed west, and said *Out there.*

I turned back to Roy John and my knees went to plain water, I fell straight down in the snow on my knees, like a man about to pray, a man calling for mercy. And that is one thing I did not want to be, a man calling for mercy. I did not want to ask for anything, not food or water, not rest, not even for my own life, and I said *Roy. Help me up, now. Don't let me stay down here.* The sheriff stood beside Roy, his shape as big as a tree, the two of them lifting me up, one on either side, and the sheriff said *Let's go, Roy.* And they led me across that snow-covered meadow with the rest of the posse behind us, me with one boot gone and walking short-legged in a sock the same meadow I'd walked across the night before to get to Judson

Church. The treeline moved up on us as if the trees were sailing in from a long way off and I could see the sleigh and the two roans snorting and blowing wet smoke in that air and I hope you're happy, Mama, because this is the first and last time you will ever hear this story, your only son shot at Rucker's Creek not five miles from his place of birth, his blood running over the ice like oil and into the water to cloud up colored like a rose and swirl away. I've always heard it said the wars of heaven are fought on righteous ground, Mama, and the godly man shall be the victor. So Roy John helped me up into that sleigh and threw a saddle blanket over me and I laid where I lay, an end to my so-called life of crime, nobody to know how lost I truly was, the man who built his own gallows in the snow, out behind the house of the Lord. I am the man who sought restitution by himself and alone in a place of his own choosing. I am the man who surrendered with one boot gone on St. Valentine's Day, the year of our Lord nineteen hundred and thirteen, with the smell of salt and woodsmoke and gunpowder in the air.

The last of this Lee family is gone now, Daddy crossed over, Rockwell Junior the robber and murderer shot down at Judson Church, and Mama, you know you died with Daddy on that covered bridge and are as gone as me and him, yes you are, sad and gone, and we have suffered for what we didn't know back when and what we couldn't find, and for what we didn't even know we'd lost. And now we are gone, we are history. We are stories nobody tells, Mama, we have disappeared back down to the bottom of that river once and for all.

Ours is the testament of snow. We are in the company of time.

THE
LOVE
OF A
GOOD
WOMAN

A NOVELLA

———

PART I

1

OUT ON THE ROAD I passed another man walking, walking as if his heart was surely broken. Go out on the road on foot and that's the kind of thing you can see, early light in your face and all your life awash in the small and unconnected minutes of your own broken heart. I had a vision shortly after I left my home: I saw myself locking a man in an icehouse, out of some vengeance and pain. It was a hot day and I put him in an icehouse and locked him in and buried the key in his garden. I left him in there to freeze in the middle of the summer. I walked away as he shouted to me for mercy and hammered at the door that had sealed him into the winter of his death. Out on the road I was given this vision to hold. I would need, I decided, a certain resolve to carry on.

■ ■ ■

My name is Delbert Keene. This is the one thing I'm rarely in doubt on. One might ask what sort of name is Keene, and I for one would be first in line to say I surely have no idea. Everybody wants to be proud of some association with their name, Chinese, Macedonian, I don't know what. I claim no flag or national privilege with my name, but I do remember once sitting outside on my father's porch saying the name *Keene* over and over, feeling just the particular shape and press of the upper lip one can find in the execution of such a peculiar little word. I was in the midst of this business, the story goes, when my father — Harry Keene, Jr. — stepped out to discover my face in some sort of contortion and decided then and there his eldest son was on the road to madness. It seems I have not let him down.

■   ■   ■

Mama always said the world was too big. Daddy said that life was too long. I didn't know about either, out on the road, one foot in front of the other, nothing but a sad-footed walker in a dream, a man that forgot the size of his past and left the wages of his present for better or worse. There was a music to the walking, just the moving that took me step by step further away from my home, my wife, my two kids. There are things a man has to do, maybe, perhaps. Things he tells himself he has to do. The trousers I was wearing were coming apart, seams going and letting go, and I wonder why it is I walked away from my home without putting on a decent pair of pants.

■   ■   ■

Now there were days around the house: God have mercy. The old lady going at me and the kids on fire and the roof lifting an inch or two each time that family took a breath and me in the middle, and I swear I'm a quiet man, an ordinary man with simple needs. It was entirely not my fault that there was no work to be found anywhere, that I had lost the one job I'd ever been able to hold on to, that my family was surviving on the spare generosity of my wife's lonely old dad. At least there was something. Nobody was starving.

■ ■ ■

My wife is named Elsa and naturally all her life everyone who has known her calls her Elsie. We married in a big spite of bliss, carried off in our own little dynamite of a passion. For the longest time I believed that such moments are what a human being lives for, a man or a woman waiting to have their feelings sent up like a Fourth of July firecracker to blow open up there under the sky and fall away in a dazzle of color. Even as I walked along the road I was thinking it is the one best reason to be alive, to be in love like that and have every little thing you ever wanted dressed up and stood on line all around the feet of this other person you adore. But time does go on. It's not that I ever discovered anything directly wrong about Elsie. But time can wear anybody out, not enough of anything. Come last Thursday and one more of Elsie's sad little tantrums and I said to myself: Now enough is enough. You stay around here, you're liable to do something drastic. You're liable to do something you regret. Naturally that was just talk, the voice that carries around in my head, going on about anything at all. I'd heard about them guys that go down to the corner for a package of smokes and nobody's ever heard of them again and I said to myself: Delbert, if it worked for them it can work for you. So on a Thursday evening — April 11, 1932 — I excused myself from the house saying I was going for a walk.

■ ■ ■

The first day out I passed through Redmond, another of these pissed-out hill towns where a real fine little house will sit right next to some abandoned cave-in from the last century. I trudged down through, looking at the houses and feeling as a matter of fact pretty damned free and on the loose, looking into the houses or nodding to old boys on their porches thinking I had no need to see anything more, no need to know anything more than what was there in front of my face. I'd hear a woman's voice inside a house, calling around in there, and I'd say: Just go on, go on and talk to the walls, see if they give a good goddamn.

I walked straight through Redmond and out onto the county road until I was alone out there, forest all around me, sun patching through in bits and pieces of heat. I was amazed how cold it could be in a shaft of shadow, just that one square of space where no sunlight fell all day. Every once in a while I'd stop to stand in a bottle of sunlight, and it was standing this way that I saw the old pickup truck rattling down the highway toward me and took the impulse to flag it down.

■   ■   ■

We had gone on a mile or two and I was trying to get my insides settled out after sitting down next to a stranger. He was the kind of old boy you see in overalls and a slouch hat, with about half the teeth in his head gone and whatever's left the color of snuff, his hands on the steering wheel looking as if they'd been beaten with a ball-peen hammer once too often. He had maybe three days' growth of white beard sticking out of his chin and neck. He drove and didn't speak a word. Nor did I. After a while I relaxed enough to start looking around at the passing scene and I happened to turn my head to see what was in the bed of the truck. I looked back at the old man, and now I had to say something, I had to ask why he was hauling the carcass of a dead horse. He drove on as if he was considering my question, as if this was something he had to think about. After maybe half a mile was gone underneath us he said: *Because it's dead*.

2

Consider the lilies of the field. And what will you see? What will come to you? What might come to pass? Don't ask me, ask my loving Elsie: she's a churchgoer. I don't mean a Holy Roller, no speaking in tongues, just a regular member of the Sunday Morning Society, sitting up in a pew, singing the heart out of those hymns like Monday will never come. I'd sit with her there, hung over for the most part, listening to the preacher run on as if the sound of his voice was the only thing that mattered in this world. Standing at the door of the church after the service he'd offer his hand like it was a blessing of some sort. Elsie would shine her eyes up into the Reverend's: *Fine sermon today, thank you so much.* Whenever I shook hands with the son of a bitch he grinned at me like he had something more than I had and was ever happy to rub it in.

The old truck wherein I'd hitched my ride battered on down the highway, and I turned away from the windshield and my thoughts to study a bit longer on the remains of the horse. A good looker, big chestnut mare, muscled like a runner. I asked the old man: *She a racer?* He worked his mouth before he said: *Was.*

So that truck was hauling ass upcountry, bound for glory for all I knew, me contemplating the situation because the fact of the matter is that it's not every day of the week an old man picks up a stranger on the road while carting the carcass of a horse. The eyes of that creature looked as if it had died suddenly and in fright, it had the eyes of something that sees the anvil coming toward its brain and knows just then that everything's coming to a close. I stared out the windshield in an attempt to clarify vision on the two-lane blacktop. Then I said to the old man: *Where you taking this thing?* He downshifted in a terrible fall-apart of a dried-up gearbox, and said: *Yonder.*

■ ■ ■

Directly on down the road we passed in view of a weathered shake house set back from the highway, a short fifty yards to my left, up on a ridge. By my count there were four women arrayed out on the porch, in various sorts of loose slips and undergarments, everybody a tad underdressed it would seem, and it made for a strange sight, this old mountain porch wedged around in gray board and bedecked with ladies in white. And the old man turns his truck right into the drive going up to this very house, pounding along through the mud ruts. I asked what he had in mind. He ground a gear in the downshift, nearly stalled, tires spun once around and caught. *Got me an appointment up here,* he said. So of course I knew the nature of his business, didn't begrudge him — a man of his age had to locate resources as he could. My sympathy, as it always had, went out to the ladies of the calling, forced by profession to entertain the likes of this old man, the sort of gentleman who murdered horses and went to the trouble of kidnapping their remains for what had to be peculiar reasons.

He came to a bad stop and slammed out. *You're welcome to come inside I reckon*, he told me. I looked up onto the porch. Three of the four ladies came to a cluster beside an upright, gazing down upon us as if they were the volunteer gatekeepers of heaven. This I was not prepared for. I had left Elsie, but not yet for another woman I supposed; though the ladies' waiting ease was a temptation and a transgression I'd come to know on more than one occasion, I thanked the old man kindly and politely declined. *I'll wait here*, I said. He simply turned and walked away, up the steps where none of the sirens made a sign they knew him or a move toward him. After a time one of them came down and approached the truck. I kept my seat and she stepped to the window: *You like to come in the house? No ma'am*, I replied, *I'm too confused for that*. She took that answer in stride and said it didn't matter what my state of mind was. *Madam*, I said, *the gentleman here who just went inside picked me up hitchhiking. And I have a concern about this horse in the back.*

She glanced a moment at the horse. *Looks to be dead*, she said.

Well, it is.

Shame. Nice horse.

It's my firm belief, I said, *that this horse was killed. With malice aforethought*. She looked back at the porch steps as if the old man was standing there so she could make an appraisal. She returned her face to my direction and said: *Well, it is possible.*

I looked up to where I could get just a slice of blue sky through the windshield. *You could always get out right here,* she said. And I replied that it was kind of nice to be riding instead of walking. *Well, then,* she told me, *don't complain about your passenger back there.*

I didn't look at her and in due course she returned to the porch without another word to me. The old man wasn't long in coming out, moving down to the truck as if he'd done nothing more than stop for a cup of coffee.

■   ■   ■

I had warned Elsie. It did not need to come to this. She knew I was near wit's end. I had said: *All right, little sister, how'd you like to just go it alone a little while, how about that?* And she says: A *hell of a lot of difference it would make.* Now I had no comeback to that except the sound of my own grievous disappointment, a sound which Miss Elsie seemed unable to hear, that and the sound of the voice in my head thinking: How could she say that, how could she let such words pass her lips? The day will come, I remember telling myself, when Miss High and Goddamn Mighty will have the very opportunity she's looking for. And the day was upon me. At which point the old man cleared his throat from behind the wheel and said: *I killed the horse.*

We drove and I'd hear myself begin a thought *The truth is* but of course the truth is I never quite knew what the truth was, and still don't. For the simple fact remains that my escapades then and since have served to cause a considerable disruption in my life and the lives of others yet I've been for the most part helpless in the matter. You might say that adventure beckoned. A doctor once told me I had a better ear than most for what he called the voices in the soul. The music of the spirit played perhaps a bit louder than it should. Lights burning when they should have been snuffed, voices working in me that sang out from the past and made plans to invade the future, like spirits on a train with a handcart full of baggage and nobody knows how they got on board in the first place but there they are, big as life and as full of noise as a five-piece band on a street corner. *Voices in the soul* — now that appealed to me and I remember thinking: Fine and dandy, as good a truth as any and I can buy it right along with the rest, one explanation being as good as another. A dreamer's ride into the tailwind of time, I told myself, a message from heaven if I ever heard one.

3

I told the old man it had occurred to me he was the culprit. He nodded without remorse. So now it was upon me: *Why, I asked, why would a man want to do a thing like this?* Again the old man drove without speaking; I had to assume he was cogitating through these pauses. Then he said: *Better than killing a man. Got it out of my system just as good.*

So I figure: Here's a new twist. You want to kill a man, but to save yourself from that you take the life of a creature this man *owns*. This idea, in a certain roughed-up framework, had its merit.

I looked behind us, over the body of the mare and down the highway. It was a wide-open stretch, clean as tomorrow, although I wondered how long before somebody would be after us, shotgun in hand. *You know,* I told the old man, *it'd be no trouble at all to trail you through this country. Everybody takes notice of what you're carrying.*

No matter, he said.

You have a plan?

After a moment he shook his head and said: *None at all.*

I took a breath and began my considerations. I considered a world where old men murder horses and young men leave their families, both young and old on a river of spite and imagining they've made a damage to be remembered by. It was a time when you become concerned with just how far salvation reaches, if indeed a sainted hand might fall down out of the gathering clouds by way of deliverance, take a fine chestnut mare in a whirlwind of dust and thereby ease an old man's fate gone awry and the ever-growing fear in his passenger of chance. The scenes rolling past my mind were what you might think — the animal's owner leaping from nowhere to hold us at gunpoint, a deputy sheriff waving us over to ask a question or two about our cargo. I deliberated upon a solution: me and the old man would stop for a drink or two, and when we walked out of the roadhouse the creature would be gone. Disappeared, taken flight. Simple as that. I was getting tired and working up an able hunger.

We are gonna get rid of this horse, I said.

The old man made no response.

It was late in the afternoon when I saw the head of a little ditch-path into the woods and suggested we explore a bit. The old man bounced into the trees. Down the trail and out of sight of the highway the path widened just enough to bring the truck around.

Let's turn to face out, I said, *back toward the road*.

The old man studied me as if I was a bigger problem for him than the horse, but went ahead with working his truck back and forth until it was pointed up toward the highway. I got out and climbed onto the bed, standing between the horse's legs, in next to its belly. The old man got out as well and looked up at me. *You got any rope?* I asked. He told me he never carried any. *Well*, I said, *we'll just have to pull the old girl off by hand.*

He studied the ground where the body would fall, as if he was gaining a sense of respect for the animal. *You wanna just leave her here?* he asked me. I nodded and said *Yes sir, we're about to divest ourselves of this beauty.*

She'll rot just a-laying here in the woods, the old man said.

So now I had to lean down, hands on my knees, let go a sigh. *My friend*, I said, *rot is all any of us can hope for. Now, if you don't mind, this here is a job for two.*

■   ■   ■

And a mighty job she was, a fierce contest into that big animal's sleek half-ton, shoving her toward the lip of the truck in what seemed no more than inches at a time. I pushed, the old man pulled as best he could and when she finally went over the edge it was twilight. Her body rolled away from the truck stiff as a board, slammed into the ground with every ounce of her weight and her legs pointing straight to the sky.

Can't we turn her on one side? The old man didn't like the look of it.

Not a pretty sight, is it?

The old man hated me, I could see it in the way he turned an eye on me just then. *Listen*, I said, *a man cannot drive about the countryside carrying a carcass as good-looking as this one right out on his truckbed.*

He hated me a while longer, and I said *I'll say a few words here, over the body. We'll send her off proper.*

So I stood up at her head (nightflies already sitting on those shiny black eyeballs) and thought: Okay, Delbert, you asked for it, you leave your home and family, the love of a good woman, and this is your payment. A dead horse comes into your life asking for disposition. You must heed the call. You're confronted by dreams of vengeance and you'll have to take it as it comes. It's this or stay home to die in a cane chair beside the kitchen sink. One way or another. *Lord!* I called into the darkening sky. The old man jumped.

I bowed my head, closed my eyes and said *Lord, we will accept that you are the —* here I sniffed and glanced at the old man, who stood hat in hands and head bowed — *that you are the God of Horses, the . . . supervisor of this horse's all-too-short life here on earth, and it falls to me to commend the soul of this creature, this . . . good animal into your care . . .*

I paused to run my tongue along my lower teeth, looking for something fitting.

. . . this good animal into your everlasting care.

The old man didn't move.

While we're at this, I said, *I might recommend a tinge of forgiveness for the old gent here who took this animal's life. In a fit of rage, I gather. I suppose we should all be forgiven our rages, am I right on this point? I guess too that while I'm at it here I should offer myself up for a little scrutiny, being as how I recently left my wife and family in the lurch. Though my good wife Elsie seems to think that my not being there is no lurch at all. I admit, Lord, I'm a prisoner of my vices, I love to take a drink now and again, I'm cursed with a touch of forgetfulness, this and that. What I might ask you at a time like this is why Elsie finds me so damned useless when I'm there and gets so wild-chicken crazy when I'm not there. If you could deliver an answer on this point I'd be grateful —*

The old man cleared his throat.

I opened my eyes and looked up: he was staring at me from

the other end of the dead horse. *You still talking about this animal here?* he asked.

I turned skyward. It was full dark, it could have been the middle of the night. *Sure,* I said. *This is all part of it.*

I scratched in front of my left ear, seeing I had lost the train in my address to God himself. I decided to bring the ceremony to an expeditious close. *So, Lord,* I said, *I believe the words they use right in here is Ashes to ashes, dust to dust.*

I thank you for your kind attention.

Amen.

PART II

1

"I BELIEVE," Delbert told Elsie as they stood in the lobby of the Wood County Courthouse, "that you're not giving me an even chance in this matter."

Elsie glared at him. "An even chance? I wonder what in your mind that might be?"

Delbert moved his head about, lifted his hands and let them fall again to his sides, shifted weight from one foot to the other.

"You've had plenty long enough," Elsie said. "I can't tolerate it anymore. You're the father of two children. Does that ever occur to you?"

"All the time. Listen, Elsie, there really was a dead horse. And an old man in over his head. I had to do something."

Elsie waited before she spoke, examining Delbert's sorrowful expression. "You know, mister, you'd claim you had to say grace over the dead body of the King of England if you thought anybody'd believe it."

Delbert pulled the brim of his fedora lower against his eyes. "That is untrue and you know it."

"I don't know what's true or not anymore, thanks to you."

Elsie glanced around the lobby. "Why don't they have a bench in here?"

Delbert turned away from Elsie to look down the corridor. "You been planning this for a while? Throw me out like an old piece of trash?"

"Don't you start in. You haven't had a paying job in two years and you act like a damned fool all over the countryside. Not to mention the little trips to nowhere you're so fond of. I'm embarrassed to look anyone in the eye."

Delbert was injured. "I'm no *fool*, madam."

"Then you tell me what you call all your carrying on. And your drinking."

"We all have our little weaknesses."

A clerk with lacquered hair emerged to call Elsie and Delbert into the judge's chambers. As they moved toward the door Delbert whispered, "You know, Judge Garr hates me. He'll send me to jail for telling a joke if he has a chance."

Elsie did not respond as they were seated across from Judge Harper Garr. The judge's spectacles gleamed over a formidable nose. He shoved a stack of papers to one side and said breezily, "So, you finally get your fill, Elsie?"

Elsie gripped her handbag firmly in her lap.

The clerk asked Delbert to remove his hat. Delbert did so, nodding at Garr. "Fine day, am I right, Judge?"

"Delbert," the judge said, "I gather you've got no lawyer."

"Well, sir, no I don't. Should I have?"

Judge Garr ignored the question. With his clerk positioned to one side with stenographic pad at the ready, the judge gazed into a meditative middle distance somewhere above and beyond Elsie's head. "Let it be known for the record," he announced, "that this is a divorce proceeding conducted at Mrs. Elsie Keene's request, pursuant to her husband's inability to provide for his family in association with a long history of erratic behavior, illegal alcohol consumption and questionable mental status."

Delbert flapped his hat against his knee. "Oh, Lord," he said. "Elsie, my dear, I hope you know what you've started here."

The judge told Delbert to be quiet, and invited Elsie to identify herself and tell her story.

Elsie offered her full name for the clerk and announced in a quavering voice that her husband was unfit for marriage or fatherhood, could not provide and might even be unsound of mind. Judge Garr, well acquainted with numerous of Delbert's local misadventures, skillfully drew forth details in his questioning. Elsie related specifics of the night Delbert had walked nude to the barn in a thunderstorm, how he talked to people who weren't there and answered her when she'd voiced no question. She detailed her continuing humiliation resulting from the Sunday her husband did a shuffling cakewalk down the aisle of the church as the entire community filed in for morning worship. All this in addition to his predilection for unannounced furloughs from family life and a penchant for homemade whiskey.

"Judge Garr?" Delbert waved his hat. "Will I be given a chance to speak here?"

Garr gazed at Delbert a moment. "All right," he said. "What's on your mind?"

Delbert turned his hat in his hands by the brim, saying that — despite a measure of truth in everything Elsie had said — he did not think of himself as either simple-minded or out of his mind. "I'm just what you might call a dreamer, Judge. I think too much. No cure for it, I reckon."

Garr nodded, leaning back into the polished black leather

of his chair. "I'm going to see about a cure," he said. "Because I'm sending you to a hospital, Delbert. I'm going to grant this divorce and put you away. You're a sick man."

Delbert forced a grin into his teeth. "I feel just fine," he said.

Elsie sat straight on her chair, stunned. She began to speak, but Judge Garr lifted a hand. "It's the least I can do."

Elsie looked at Delbert, her mouth open, and back at the judge, who stood, duty discharged, every inch a scholar and a gentleman. "Don't thank me, my dear. I'm only too happy to help."

The next and last time Delbert left home a sheriff's deputy waited to deliver him to the asylum at Spencer in accordance with the judge's ruling. Cardboard suitcase tied once around with a length of twine, hugging and kissing his two children on the front porch, Delbert departed with the air of a man drafted into a righteous war and off to heroic ends. He walked to the passenger side of the deputy's car and got in. His son and daughter waved gaily, thinking their father would be home soon enough. Elsie shadowed the door before she turned away.

2

At the asylum Delbert led a peaceful existence in a knee-length hospital gown. He was a zephyr in broadcloth, miming for the vacant simpletons and loose-eyed madmen he lived with, imitating them with a painful accuracy looked upon with clinical disapproval by the institution's staff. Delbert's own predicament seemed beyond anybody's particular interest; for respite he would rise at dawn to sit cold in a metal chair on the asylum's vast pillared portico and watch the light rise out of the earth. That time of day reminded him of what he imagined the birth of the world was like, a place cleared for the advent of birds, its people lying asleep on their sides in forests full of new wisteria and lilac and dogwood.

When Delbert looked up from his chair on the verandah, the morning sky was soft as an inland sea.

3

It was clear to the asylum's supervising physicians that Mr. Delbert Keene was neither insane nor demented, nor otherwise deranged in any form they could account for. He was discharged in the summer of 1932 after less than a three-month stay, escorted to the gate and left there on the roadside. With two dollars in his pocket — compliments of the state of West Virginia — and no specific destination, Delbert carried a corner of concern for what might become of him, and when the Victor Brothers Tent Show and Mystic East Menagerie caught up to him on the road he was more than happy to accept a ride going anywhere.

■ ■ ■

The man who gave Delbert the ride beckoned from behind the wheel of a flatbed delivery van. There was a wooden box big enough to camp in built onto the bed of the truck, painted over in a myriad swirl of frenzied colors, none of which Delbert could name. They seemed to be colors from another language, lacing billows and banners, interweaving faces and bodies and clothing that all spoke to Delbert of erotic mystery and uncivilized gaiety, and he stood a moment, gawking.

"You gonna get in or am I driving on?" The man at the wheel was easily past sixty years. The big face he leaned toward Delbert bore the worn-in wages of more than carnival life. On the seat beside him was a small black dog.

Delbert got in beside the driver and the dog. The driver said nothing, inching his van back onto the highway in line with other such vans ahead of and behind him. Delbert propped his suitcase on his knees. "Snake-oil boys?" he said.

The driver watched the truck ahead, which had blue elephants coiled together by tails and trunks on its back end. The little dog stared solemnly at Delbert. "We'll sell a little patent medicine if we can," the driver said. "That what you mean?"

"Coulda used me a touch of elixir," Delbert said philosophically. "Back there where I was."

"Where were you?"

"Spencer State Hospital for the Insane." Delbert made the announcement as if he were declaring his graduation from a fine university.

The driver gave a glance in Delbert's direction. "So why'd they let you out?"

"I'm not insane," Delbert said, smiling like a postcard cherub.

The driver nodded. "I should have figured that."

There was a short silence and Delbert said, "There's no elephants in that truck up there, is there?"

"Nah," the driver said. "We lost our one elephant. Up in Pennsylvania. Froze to death."

"You left your elephant out?"

"One of them late spring freezes. Hard freeze and it did the old girl in. Too bad — that's money out of pocket for the owner of this show."

"Shouldn't have left her out at night."

"So why'd they put you in?" the driver asked.

"In where?"

The driver imitated Delbert's lofty tone of a moment before. "The Spencer State Hospital for the Insane," he said. "You told me why they let you out, but not why they put you in."

The little dog continued to gaze at Delbert, who returned the stare. "This your dog?"

"Yes indeed," the driver said. "This here's my old friend Low." The dog looked around at the driver when it heard its name, appreciative.

"Low?"

"As in low-down. In that he stands low to the ground. He's another 'bo, just like me. Wandered in about two years ago."

Delbert nodded at the dog. "Low, pleased to meet you. I'm Delbert Keene."

Low flicked his stub tail against the seat, carrying on with his study of Delbert's face.

"He's the serious sort," Delbert said.

"Well, does a clown good to have a serious sidekick."

"You a clown with this show?"

"That and whatever else comes up that needs doing. But mainly clowning. A funny suit and facepaint."

"And people laugh at you," Delbert said.

"You are a little touched, aren't you?"

Delbert was offended. "Why'd you say that? I'm behaving myself. I'm minding my manners."

"I say I'm a clown and you say people laugh at me. Well, I damn well *hope* so."

"I was just thinking too loud," Delbert told the clown.

The caravan wound down a hill south of the town of Bellington. At a hairpin — the trucks gearing back to a crawl — Delbert could see the entire train: all the vans painted in wild array, animal cages chained to flatbeds, a panel truck with WA-HOO BITTERS on the side in a flagrant cursive, each vehicle easing around the roadbend in turn and downshifting for the steep grade ahead.

"So where around here," Delbert said, "could we pick up an elephant at a good price?"

The driver took a deep breath. "Brother," he said, "I better take you back where I found you."

■　■　■

Delbert accepted a draft from the clown's flask, feeling a fine gratitude with the first swallow, savoring the heat. "My, my," he said quietly, "that tastes just like moonlight." He took another sip and recapped the flask, handing it back. "I do appreciate your picking me up."

The clown said, "You looked like you needed it."

The caravan bumped over a railroad crossing. Delbert looked off to his right, down a reach of vacant track. "You know," he said, "when I was a kid I loved to go out walking the railroad tracks."

"Where you from?"

"Boaz," Delbert said.

"West Virginia?"

"I gather you're unaware of my native metropolis."

The clown sucked his teeth. "Don't believe I've ever heard of it."

"Not to worry. No need to hear about it." Delbert watched the two-lane highway disappear beneath them. "Never could figure out why more than one family stopped there to begin with. But there we were."

"Country's filled with places like that. It's my theory that folks just get tired. Can't move no more."

"Maybe that's it."

"So you walked the tracks?"

Delbert nodded. "When I was a boy. Out there in search of a little peace and quiet. A little touch of privacy." He slid his valise from his lap, into the space in front of his legs, and lifted Low onto his knees. "There was this one day I went out — I was walking south, I remember, downriver — it was the middle of a summer."

The clown held the truck into a long curve. Delbert scratched Low's wiry chest and said, "It was hot. The way a morning seems to rise right into that kind of heat you can get down by a river. You might know what I'm talking about."

"I'm listening," the clown said.

"I'd go out walking the tracks and wait for the first train of the morning to come riding toward me like a damned bullet out of a gun. Those trains were whirlwinds, ready to bring down the sky, and I'd crouch there beside the tracks letting the roar build inside my belly until it was gone and I'd realize I'd been holding my breath and didn't even know it."

Low clicked his stub tail back and forth a few times, panting.

"Anyway," Delbert said, "there was this morning, middle of

July, I was maybe fourteen years old at the time and I'd headed out south for a warehouse downstream I frequented. This place had a pier stilted out over the mudflats; I'd hide under the pier when the barge came in and listen to the rivermen talking up above my head. Always the same boat, the *Colonel Blue*, and back then I thought there really was a Colonel Blue who'd be sitting up there in the wheelhouse, he'd be smoking a pipe and have this little cap tilted at an angle befitting his rank and authority." Delbert paused, lifting his chin toward the windshield. "Colonel Blue, I always figured, was the man in command of all the waters of this earth."

The clown drove on in silence. Delbert took a breath and continued.

"It was this particular July day that I reached the warehouse to find it deserted, locked up, no barge coming or going, no sign of anything about to happen, and *quiet*. So there I was in the midst of just such a day, up on the warehouse loading dock, coming around the side where the boxcars lined up, when I saw him lying there on the track."

The clown kept his eyes on the road ahead. "Him?"

"Eustace Ledbetter. Friend of my father's."

"Dead?"

"Oh, God." Delbert shook his head, lost in the remorse of memory. "Mr. Ledbetter looked as if he'd just come from an appointment with Satan himself. He was athwart the track, arms and legs twisted out in the most awful contortions and his face the color of my daddy's dandelion wine. I could just see one eye and it was half-open with the eyeball rolled back and here I'm talking about a bad man's *stare*, looking right at *me*, Delbert Keene, nothing but a lad of fourteen, looking straight *through* me."

Delbert ruffled Low's ears. "You know, at first I was sorry for ol' Ledbetter, he was a nice enough man, good with a joke, ready with an easy smile, and then it came over me, this terrible *feeling* — there I was, just a boy and alone on the tracks with a corpse, and I thought: Not a good thing, never a good thing, no sir. I would pay, I felt sure, I would pay with every manner of bad dream and hell-bent vision. I'd come up with pestilence, my teeth'd blow out of my mouth when I sneezed, I'd have worms in my hair. I'd dream about coffins and burials. And what if I was *blamed* for this? Jesus! Well you know I turned and ran, ran for all my young heart was worth, back up the tracks and then I ducked out to the riverbank and down into a little underbrush and just sat there with the river water lapping the mud as peaceful as you please and the entire rest of the world sitting pretty and I asked myself what I had done that deserved such a punishment, what sin I had committed that merited a curse of this dire magnitude . . . and I thought about the story my grandma loved to tell, about how dead men can talk. She said the dead might rise to tell their tales in the proper situation, and you know just then I wished it were true. Eustace Ledbetter was the one soul who could clear my name, pronounce me free of guilt, let everybody know I was only an innocent who had wandered into a mistaken fate. I sat there a while longer until I knew I couldn't put off going home any longer. I'd have to go home and tell my daddy I'd come on the body of his friend lying across the railroad tracks. So I headed back home and you know I took my time, feeling all the way that I was somehow to blame for what had happened, that I would in some way have to explain the whole thing. By the time I reached my back door I had drawn enough courage together to mount the steps, and I walked into my mama's kitchen and all the eyes in that room turned to look at me, including those of Mr. Eustace Ledbetter, who was seated at the table across from my daddy."

The old clown laughed without making a sound, moving his shoulders up and down. Delbert looked at him seriously. "So what'd you do?" the clown asked.

"I lifted a finger," Delbert said, "pointed at him and said *You're dead.* Whereupon my mama chastises me for being impolite to a guest and I say *He is dead, Mama. I saw him down in the yards, dead as I'm standing here in front of you.* So Ledbetter tries to look at me but he's so drunk he can't, and he says *I feel pretty dead, matter of fact.* My daddy says that Ledbetter just stopped in on the way home and about that time Ledbetter proceeds to fall asleep sitting straight up, snoring right out loud, and I tell my daddy I *thought* he was dead. At which point Daddy proceeds to throw a temper on account of my claiming Ledbetter was dead, and I knew I'd better make my way out of that kitchen and the situation I was in and I just slipped backward, right out the door I'd come through not two minutes before. But I learned one thing from that experience."

"And what might that be?"

"My grandma was right," Delbert said in a confidential tone. "Dead men *can* talk."

The clown laughed heartily over the steering wheel, downshifting for an upgrade. Delbert stared through the windshield. "My wife Elsie never did believe that story," he said.

"Your wife?" The clown looked incredulous.

"She said I'd made it up."

"You got a wife?"

"She left me. In a manner of speaking."

The clown grinned at Delbert. "How could she leave you in a manner of speaking? She did or she didn't."

"She left me in spirit," Delbert allowed.

"Ah." The clown nodded. "I've had similar troubles."

"Then you know of what I speak."

"I guess I do. Maybe I do." Then the clown said, "My name's Wilson Stinchcomb." He pushed his right hand across from the steering wheel for Delbert to shake. "I did like that tale you told. You looking for work?"

■　　■　　■

Late that afternoon the Victor Brothers Tent Show parked in a pasture at one end of the main street of Paradise, West Virginia. The field was full of animals, chained to tent stakes or tethered with guide ropes. Side tents were going up to house the concessionaires. The fortuneteller hung colored banners — indigo, white, cardinal red — from the back of her wagon. Roustabouts winched the big-top center pole into position as Wilson Stinchcomb found a plot of grass for his truck and came to a halt. He shut off the motor and turned in his seat to face Delbert. "You got the looks of a Red Indian, I'd say," Wilson said.

Delbert was amazed. "I've never even seen an Indian," he said.

Wilson grinned. "Well, sir, you're about to become one. Follow me." Wilson got out of the truck, whistling Low after him. Delbert sat where he was.

After a moment he heard the back door of the truck's box open and Wilson's voice: "Come on!"

Delbert got out and went to the rear of the truck. Wilson was standing there with an Indian war bonnet. "Here you go, Chief Delbert, try this on."

Delbert drew back. "Where'd you get that damned thing?"

"Pitchman's stand in Gallup, New Mexico," Wilson said. "Put it on. Let me have a look at you."

Delbert sat the bonnet on his head, smoothing the feathers away from either side of his face.

Wilson nodded in pure appreciation. "The living image," he said.

"Of what?"

"Of my assistant." And Delbert heard about what Wilson called the advance team, two men that went into a town with three flats of patent medicine, some posters, and ready handshakes. Wilson advised that it was another little bit of advertising for the main show. It was, he told Delbert, just like running for political office.

Delbert was warming to the idea.

"You're the Indian brave that, you might say, lends credence to the bitters," Wilson said.

"Bitters?"

"Wa-hoo Bitters, my good man."

Delbert felt his smile open. "Wa-hoo Bitters, that traditional remedy of my tribe? Handed down through ten generations on my mother's side? Which, in fact, is a watered-down batch of nothing much at all?"

Wilson gave one of his silent laughs. "Boy, you don't even need rehearsing," he said.

Delbert readjusted his headdress, making sure the feather train cascaded properly down his back. "When do we leave?"

Wilson lifted an arm toward the front of the truck. "After you, Chief."

■　■　■

Paradise proved to be something less than a flower-enameled Eden: a decrepit collection of dogtrots and shanties fringing outward from a stand-up stretch of saloon, general merchandise store, garage; a single paved street in random disrepair. The sidewalk fronting saloon and store was an elevated plank runway of the sort seen more commonly fifty years before. Wilson drove through town once, surveying, before turning around to come back through.

"This here's Indian country all right," Delbert said.

"Must make you feel right at home," Wilson told him as he parked in front of the general store. He paused behind the wheel before he said, "Well, let's see if we can attract any attention."

Delbert said, "You worried about attention? With me in this get-up?"

Wilson looked at him, shrugging. "You never know, boy. Some of these little towns . . ."

Delbert lifted his right hand in a gesture that seemed meaningful. "Wait for me here."

"Where you going?"

"In that store there. Let's see how much attention I can draw."

Delbert walked into the store, erect in a mock dignity. The storekeeper and two women musing over eggs looked up and stared.

"I come in peace," Delbert announced.

■　　■　　■

Wilson Stinchcomb and Chief Delbert returned to the showgrounds some two hours later, having sold two flats of bitters, put a handbill in every window they had time to find, and been personally welcomed by the mayor of Paradise. Delbert developed his story, The Last of My People, as he demonstrated the bitters to all comers, immediately recognizing a savory combination of grain alcohol and caramel flavoring, growing ever drunker as he and Wilson Stinchcomb moved from one presentation to another. *Wa-hoo Bitters*, Delbert announced several times over, *is absolutely guaranteed to bring a restful yet joyous sensation to both body and soul. It has been used among my people for generations. And that,* he intoned reverently, *is God's own truth.*

In the Paradise saloon Chief Delbert accepted a double shot of Southern Comfort on the house, lifted his glass to the men congregated there and extended his invitation to them on behalf of the Victor Brothers themselves, that the good gentlemen of Paradise — and their fine families — might attend the once-in-a-lifetime performance scheduled for that very evening. Wilson lifted his glass in tandem, touching Delbert's in gracious ceremony. "Let me second the Chief's invitation," he called out.

Wilson and Delbert gazed at each other solemnly, and downed the whiskeys.

■   ■   ■

After his afternoon's work in Paradise, Delbert was a bit unsteady as Wilson painted his face for the evening show.

"You're sure about this now?" Delbert widened his eyes and brought them back to a squint. "You know," he mumbled through puckered lips, "I've only actually seen clowns in a circus one time. Couldn't have been more than twelve years old. And I didn't have a good seat."

Wilson stepped back. "What exactly are you doing with your face?"

"Rehearsing," Delbert said.

Wilson resumed his work.

"Being twelve years old and having that bad seat, well" — Delbert shook his head — "you can see I'm at a disadvantage here."

"This works better when you shave," Wilson said, smearing a palm of white over Delbert's left cheek.

"What would you have of me, kind sir?" Delbert jacked his jaw up and down.

"I'd have you hold still."

"What I mean is, how is this done?"

"After what I saw this afternoon, I'd say you don't need any lessons. God knows what'd happen if I put you in a turban." Wilson worked a broad red line around Delbert's mouth. "Just take your lead from me," he said. "Follow your instincts."

"What happened to your last assistant?"

"He left me."

Delbert stared straight ahead, trying to hold his head in one position. "He left you, in a manner of speaking?"

Wilson stopped painting and looked into Delbert's color-rimmed eyes. "In a manner of speaking, yes. This would go along faster if you could manage to shut up."

"I believe," Delbert murmured, "I may have overdone it a bit on the Wa-hoo back there."

"A little black coffee, you'll be good as new."

"Wilson, when do I meet the illustrious Victor Brothers?"

"There are no Victor Brothers, Chief. Never have been. That's just a name."

Delbert drew his face away from Wilson's hand, pushing his

forehead higher by an inch, an elaborate surprise. "Just a name! I beg your pardon, sir!"

Wilson crinkled a grin into his tumbledown face. "That's a good look there," he said. "You better use that one in the ring."

Delbert relaxed his forehead. "I'll give it a try."

"Now shut up," Wilson said, returning to work with the facepaint, and so it was that Delbert Keene became a clown, in the town of Paradise, under the tutelage of the small-time master Wilson Stinchcomb. The Victor Brothers Show took Delbert on as "Keno the Clown," paid him a pocket wage from the till as they traveled south across that summer through West Virginia and Kentucky and into Tennessee, Delbert perfecting the art that Wilson said he was born to: the sad man's disguise, the drunkard's revenge. He worked most of the one-night backtown stands there were, and when the show's owner rented five train cars to take the show west by rail, Delbert signed on with a regular salary. He walked the noontime parades that announced the circus's arrival, racing from one side of a street to the other, teasing children, giving away candy, honking the horn in his pocket when he opened his mouth. At every show yellow-haired children in flannel leaned forward to see Delbert produce the live white mouse he carried in his pocket, to watch him pull Japanese fans and colored pencils out of his ears, squirt himself in the face from the red carnation on his bib. A rumpled corsage bloomed under a polka-dot bandanna: Delbert bowed and handed it soberly to a grandmother. He looked amazed, dissolute, shocked, coy, brokenhearted, fell on his nose and was on the road by midnight, the rest of the troupe asleep as Delbert sat up and smoked at a dark window, his eyebrows still white from the grease pencil, a litany of town names sliding by on cornices of empty stations and Delbert's reflection a fractured glimpse of shadow in the window, afloat with the mournful train.

4

"After midnight," Delbert said, "and the boy's still dreaming."

The bartender said, "How's that?"

"Just taking note of the time," Delbert told him.

The bartender stopped his wiping in front of Delbert. "You're not from around here, are you?"

Delbert grinned. "No sir," he said, "I'm from one hell of a long way off. I'm from Pago Pago. I'm from the dark side of the moon. How about yourself?"

The bartender looked at Delbert, serious and pitying, did not speak, carried on with his wiping.

"Fact is," Delbert said to his whiskey glass, "the world don't know a goddamn thing about obsession. Not a goddamn thing. Nothing about passion either. How can a man have hope in a world where passion and obsession don't have no place?"

The bartender retired to a stool at the far end of the bar and watched Delbert.

"It so happens I've got the God-given gift of making people laugh. Now when a man gets him a God-given gift it's his responsibility to carry on with it. To live within the thing he does the best. And it's the responsibility of the world to see that he does just that, not let him waste time on all manner of other nonsense." Delbert looked up, squinting in the direction of the bartender. "This ain't no drunk talk," he said. "So stop looking at me that way."

"If this ain't drunk talk," the bartender said, "then I'd like to know what the hell it is."

Delbert stood down from the stool, nearly fell, gripped the bumper on the bar for support. "This," he said, "is the simple goddamn truth."

"Watch the language," the bartender said. "Still got ladies in the place."

"They can hear the truth too," Delbert said. "Won't hurt 'em a bit."

"And what might the truth be?"

"The truth is, this life don't have no beginning or end. You notice that? Can't remember your beginning, and after it's all over you won't remember that either. The only thing that counts is what's in the damn middle."

The bartender started to laugh.

Delbert blinked at him. "Maybe I didn't get that quite right."

"I don't know if you did or didn't," the bartender said, still laughing.

Delbert took a breath, seriously watching the bartender's laughter. "I believe I'll go get me some rest."

The bartender nodded. "You do that."

"It's my understanding," Delbert said, pointing toward the door, "that the promised land lies just beyond."

"I wouldn't be a bit surprised," the bartender told him.

5

Climbing, moving with the same considered deliberation of muscle he used in the circus ring, Delbert remembered the recent past in slow hitches out of an Irish whiskey haze, handholds one over the other up the rock face. He had decided that this particular alcohol frenzy would best be atoned for by climbing the eastern cliff-face of the rounded-off mountain in southern Virginia he had looked at for four weeks from his cell window. Delbert had been arrested in a saloon a month earlier when he slapped an astonished barkeep to the floor with a fresh-caught river bass another patron was carrying in a pail of ice: the whack of the fish on the bartender's cheeks and Delbert's wild laughter before the local police took him to a cell. Delbert advised an aged magistrate that the barkeep had cast unjust aspersions on certain members of the circus profession, and drew thirty days on charges of public drunkenness and assault. He took to singing "The Old Rugged Cross" in his cell, over and over, slowly, plaintively, teaching himself harmony on a concertina left among the effects of a prisoner who had died in the same cell some time before. Wilson Stinchcomb was sent to advise Delbert that the show was moving on; if he could catch up when he was out of jail he would be welcome back. Delbert bowed deeply. Wilson cursed him with affection.

Halfway up the rock and the ledges grew smaller, inch-wide avenues of blue-veined mica inlay and handholds nothing more than wrinkles as he spread-eagled, at one point laughing flat against the cool rock. He moved up into an area of wet stone and slipped, splaying arms and legs to maintain purchase with the dry holds that would carry him, pressing his cheek into the seep. The water was sweet and fresh as ice. Delbert caught his breath, easing away the momentary fright. Looking up, the mountainside reared and the sky rode down and the meeting between stone and unclouded blue seemed like a glorious event, the border where angels surely sang.

Below, a wide country drew away, a haze of ripe green and the silent line of a single river.

Delbert carried on with the climb, entertaining himself creating names for the mountain: Wild Man's Notion, Delbert's Folly, Loser's Delight. Near the summit he felt himself flagging and pervaded by doubt. At an arm's length above he could see the loose hair of moss and soil overhanging the precipice, a root piercing the high lip of the mountainside. He tested the root for weight-bearing; it brought his head into the moss. Pebbles skittered away. Delbert lifted into a thicket of raspberry and daylight. He was heaving for breath.

On the grass-lined knoll of the summit two lovers took their pleasure, the woman embroiled in petticoats, the man between her legs with expensive trousers at his knees, his shirttail in the wind. When he heard Delbert punch through into the raspberry, the man turned around suddenly, stunned to see a human face where one could not possibly be.

"Jesus Christ," the man said. The woman leaned up on her right elbow.

Delbert was contrite. "Sorry," he said. "Kindly forgive me."

The man said, "Are you out of your mind?"

Delbert smiled sweetly. "That's a point of contention there, sir," he said.

6

On a train heading south Delbert thought of the past as if it were a long border trembling in the wavering light of his days, time's own mirage. Something forgotten or wasted back there, he decided, and what, dear Lord, might it have been? *Once I was a boy, and where is that boy now?* He squinted at the black window, intent on the resurrection of a boy's face, a boy he would know, waving knee-deep from a creek, making through daylight, grinning into the everlasting. Delbert saw nothing of the kind. He turned away from the window: in the overhead rack across the aisle a punched-in felt hat was the shape of an airplane in flight. The train moaned into a turn, a thin whistle wheezing deep in its body. Delbert turned back to his window. Failures of vision, he thought, surround us.

7

The woman, when Delbert saw her, was more a girl than otherwise, walking the edge of the circus camp, holding the baby. She walked straight and hard, not looking around, which Delbert found curious. Everybody looked at a circus camp — anyone would stop and watch and smile at a world where clowns and dwarfs played pinochle on sheets thrown out over anthills; where a solitary musician served up intricate cornet meditations, offered to the empty air from the back step of a painted wagon. She did not stop to look and was dressed as if she were a hundred years old — the long skirt, the scarf. Delbert crossed the inside of the camp so he could stand in her path. As she approached he bowed, the courtly gesture. "Madam," he intoned.

Now she stopped, looking at him. He rose and their eyes met and Delbert said, "Perhaps I can be of service?"

"I doubt it."

"I notice a lady with a child walking like you are and I think maybe you might be in need of assistance."

"I'm making my way," she said.

Delbert was in full clownface but still in street clothes. The show was at hand; it was no more than an hour before the ringmaster would start the procession into the tent.

"I'm taking my baby to the doctor."

"Bad?" Delbert asked.

"I don't know. Not yet, I guess. I'm not gonna sit out in a cabin and wait when I should have started off and I don't know why I'm telling you any of this anyway. I can't even see who you are."

Delbert looked into the palm of his right hand as if it would be invisible. "Oh," he said, nodding. "My face. Well, be assured that I am indeed under this paint."

She looked briefly back in the direction of the big-top. "Don't you have to go to work?"

"In due course, I guess I do. I was thinking of lending a hand. Take you in to the doctor a bit faster."

"I'll get there."

Delbert lifted his hands. "Stay right where you are. If you would. I can borrow a car. I'll borrow a car and you tell me which way to steer." Delbert was suddenly ebullient. "We'll have you there in no time!"

She stared after Delbert as he trotted away into the profusion of a circus gathering forces for an afternoon show. She stood, waiting, and nobody took notice of her, a woman with a baby at the edge of the grounds. She watched a boy lead a saddled camel toward the big-top, then heard the car horn as Delbert skidded a road-weary Chevrolet sedan out into pasture grass. He braked and waved her over.

Hesitating at the door, she thought about going to town in an automobile driven by a clown. He grinned and his mouth seemed to fly apart with the wide bar of red around his lips. "Climb in and I'll give you a ride fit for a queen."

She held the baby tighter. "I don't need no ride fit for a queen. I just want to go to town."

Delbert bobbed his head. "Purely my pleasure," he said.

She got in next to Delbert, and now her baby woke and began to cry. Delbert put the car in gear to lurch off across the pasture: she held fast to the door as the faces of passersby loomed. Delbert punched the horn and gave no quarter to the growing crowd.

"God!" she called out.

"Not to worry!" Delbert yelled. "We'll have you there in no time!" The car hit a ditch and she thought the bottom would go and they would fall forever. Delbert pushed through and onto the dirt road in front of the big-top, turning right. "It's the other way!" she shouted.

"The other way, yes ma'am!" Delbert yanked the car in a wide circle, bouncing off the road onto grass. The wheel turned loose in his hands for a moment and the car lurched forward into a roped-off enclosure holding six horses ready to promenade, white saddles on their backs and shakos between their ears. Delbert leaned the wheel full to the left as a yardboy came running toward the car and the horses shied back in disarray on their guide rope, turning over water buckets, one mare rearing fire-eyed to threaten the hood of the car. The woman clung to her child and Delbert headed out onto the road. He looked to the rearview mirror to see other clowns running after him, waving and shouting; a man in a suit gestured and was clearly outraged. James Faulk, the circus manager, stood behind them in the center of the road in his ringmaster's outfit, watching his automobile disappear. The baby was howling.

"Sorry, there," Delbert said. "Seems I've frightened the child."

The woman sat, staring straight ahead of her.

"It'll be fine, now," Delbert said. "Just took me a wrong turn back there."

"You didn't borrow this car."

"Sure I did!" Delbert leaned back in his seat. "I'll bring it back. Have to, to get back to the show."

She worked to calm her baby, wiping its nose with a corner of her shawl. "I mean you didn't *ask* for it. Lord."

"What's your name?"

"Maybe you better let me out right here and take this car on back."

"And then you wouldn't get your baby to the doctor. Come on now, what's your name?"

She opened her dress and put the baby to her breast. "Everybody was pretty upset back there at the circus," she said.

Delbert nodded. "They'll get over it. Doctor'll have a look at your baby and we'll be back here in no time. You can see the show for free."

"We won't be back before the circus begins."

Delbert glanced at her. "How far we have to go?"

"Seven miles."

"You were going to walk seven miles?"

"I already come five."

They drove on a bit before Delbert said, "I gather I'm headed in the right direction."

She turned the baby to her other breast. Delbert stole a look: a little nipple stiff with the child's sucking, wet with milk. "Just keep on," she said. "You'll see the turn up ahead. Points you right down toward town." She looked around the interior of the car. "Did you tell me who you are?"

"Delbert Keene, at your service. Otherwise and sometimes

known as Keno, one of the jesters for that hippodrome back there."

She blinked several times, considering the information. Then she said, "I'm Rosalinda Breedlove."

"Rosalinda." Delbert sang the name: *Rosalinda.* "My, my. Now there's a name."

She shifted the child to her shoulder, patting its back.

"You think we ought to go faster?" Delbert asked earnestly.

"No sir!"

Delbert looked down at the speedometer. "We're going right about twenty-six miles per hour."

She shook her head. "That's just fine. I got a baby to think about here. After that show you put on back up the road."

Delbert grinned, accepting her remark as a congratulation. "Wasn't that nice? Had 'em going every which way."

Rosalinda studied the side of Delbert's face. "You thought that was fun?"

"Well." Delbert shrugged. "For us. I guess not for your baby."

"For *you!* I was scared to death."

Delbert looked at her but she could read no expression under the facepaint. "I do apologize then," he said. "No harm intended."

They approached a sign with an arrow, indicating the town of Hornbeak to be three miles further on, bearing left. Delbert took the direction. "You know where this doctor's office is?"

"There's only one. He keeps it in his house."

Delbert smiled. "I guess you'll direct me once we get into town."

She did not answer then, rocking the baby. Delbert leaned forward to look up into the trees passing overhead. "I love that," he said. "The way the trees'll slide over you, and you just watch all that green coming and going, like it's right in front of your eyes. Like a summer river."

Rosalinda asked how long he'd been with the circus. "Some three years all together," Delbert told her. "Had me a little trouble up in Virginia and lost a show. Ran into this one by accident and joined up. An unperfect actor on the stage, as the man said."

"What man?"

"Shakespeare, I'm told."

"Is he one of the clowns with your show?"

"Not to my knowledge," Delbert said, braking Faulk's Chevrolet and rolling past small clean frame houses, rose arbors, heavy willows.

Rosalinda looked out her window. "I don't have no money," she said quietly.

Delbert had no money himself, having left the circus grounds as he had. "You better tell me where the doctor is."

"Just keep on. He's at the other end of town."

"This doctor won't work without payment?"

"I don't know. I hate to go in there with nothing. But there's no other way."

Delbert's eye was caught by the Farmers and Merchants Bank and he turned into a parking space in front of the building.

"What're you doing?" Rosalinda asked.

"I'm going in here and see if I can get a loan," Delbert said.

"I believe you're straight off your head," Rosalinda told him.

Delbert drew a sober breath and tapped the steering wheel.

She blinked at him. "I'm getting out. I'm walking the rest of the way."

"Well, now, wait. Just give me a minute in here." Delbert pushed back against his seat. "That's the damn trouble with this world. Nobody willing to give anything a try." He let the steering wheel have one more firm knuckle-tap. "What's the harm in asking?"

"Like you asked for this car?"

"I *know* the man who owns this car. He knows I'll be back. Now do you want some help or not?" Delbert looked at her baby a moment before he rocked out of the car, closed the door and leaned down into the open window. "Won't be a minute," he said.

■   ■   ■

The interior of the Farmers and Merchants Bank was a cool amber, latticed in filtered sunlight. There were no customers in the bank as Delbert stepped directly to the black bars at the teller's window. She was a round-faced girl with what Delbert took to be a drop of Indian blood. Her chestnut hair was severely bobbed. She stared solemnly at Delbert without reaction.

"Excuse the makeup," Delbert said softly, leaning toward the bars. "I'm dressed for work."

"Dressed for work," she repeated flatly.

"Yes ma'am. I've dropped in to inquire about a loan."

"A loan?"

"Yes." Delbert nodded. "You see, I got a little girl out in the car with a sick baby. We could use a little extra just now."

The teller stared.

"Whatever you got there in that top drawer'd be just fine," Delbert said.

The teller said nothing.

Delbert shifted to lean on his left elbow, assuming an intimate and conspiratorial tone. "This loan's guaranteed by Mr. Hud Raney, owner of the Raney Brothers Circus, just a spit and a holler up the road there. In fact, I'll personally guarantee you and your loved one free admission."

"Are you armed?"

Delbert laughed, seeing she had the wrong idea. He lifted both hands into the air. "Honey, I got two arms. Thank the Lord, right?"

"I'm gonna scream for help," the teller said in a savage undertone.

"There's no need to scream," Delbert said gently. "I mean no harm. I'm in the circus, down the road. This facepaint here's just part of the job. I'm not trying to scare you with it."

"That's some kind of disguise!"

Delbert looked around the bank. He saw nobody. He was becoming exasperated. "Listen, I've taken on the responsibility of a sick child —"

"That's the worst story I ever heard," the teller barked.

"It's no damn *story!*" Delbert had raised his voice. He let go a long breath. "All right, now. Listen, you need guidance on this and I'll give you some." He walked to the end of the teller desk and through the swinging door, behind the black wrought iron to the teller's position.

"Get away!" she shouted, pulling back.

Delbert drew open the cash drawer, and turned to point at her. "Now you're being plain silly, you know that? I said this was a loan, didn't I? If the manager were here we could discuss it like gentlemen. I'll have it back to you in the morning. Every damn cent." Delbert took a random handful from one of the partitions in the cash drawer. "Try to extend a helping hand in this world and you gotta do everything yourself. Christ." He stuffed the cash in a side pocket of his coat and banged through the swinging door and marched across the lobby. As he left he turned and yelled back to the teller: "I got kids of my own, you know!"

Outside Delbert saw immediately that Faulk's car was empty. Rosalinda and her child were in view, about fifty yards down the street. He got in and started the engine. As he wrenched into reverse, he saw the teller watching him from the bank's front window. Delbert gave her the biggest smile he could manage, and a cheery wave.

On the street he stopped the car beside Rosalinda. "Get in!" he yelled.

She paused at the window: he could see only the middle of her body, the baby clutched in her arms. "Come on," Delbert said. "I'm not gonna have the ghost of a dead child following me around the rest of my life."

8

"My God," the doctor said from the top of the stairwell. He stood half in shadow: Delbert could see him from the waist down, gold watch chain curving a plump half-moon around his belly, rumpled pinstripe trousers, big cuffs and black brogans.

"Sir," Delbert called up, "we have us a sick child here."

"You're painted like a clown." The doctor's voice emanated from the darker upper reaches of the house.

"Well, sir," Delbert said, grinning, "I am at that. Professional attire, you might say."

The doctor did not respond, stepping slowly into the soft light at the bottom of the stairs. He was wearing burgundy braces with shirtsleeves rolled to the elbow.

"You look tired, sir," Delbert said.

The doctor put his hands in his pockets, moving his lips over his teeth. "You're painted like a clown," he said very quietly.

"I'm with the circus," Delbert said. "Raney Brothers Tent

Show." Delbert pushed his thumb at the doctor's front door, as if the big-top were pitched in front of the house.

"So I gathered," the doctor said.

Delbert touched the sullen Rosalinda Breedlove on the shoulder. "This young woman was in need of rescue," he said. "You might say I rose to the occasion."

The doctor blinked at the child in Rosalinda's arms. "Rescuing people," he said after a moment, "will be the death of you, my friend."

There was a rustle on the stairway. The doctor's wife called from above. "Ed? Everything okay?"

The doctor had stepped closer to Rosalinda and studied the baby, keeping his hands pocketed. "Sick baby," he said. His wife moved down the stairs, stopping when she saw Delbert.

Delbert nodded. "Ma'am," he said. "Good afternoon."

"He's with the circus," the doctor murmured, now laying his palm against the baby's chest.

The doctor's wife recovered quickly, and smiled. "You get called away suddenly from work?"

"Well, ma'am," Delbert said, "matter of fact that *is* what happened. This young lady here was on her way in to see the doctor, so I thought I'd just give her a lift."

"In a stolen car," Rosalinda growled.

"Borrowed car," Delbert said, congenial as a salesman.

"Well." The doctor exhaled heavily. "Follow me."

Delbert stepped aside, indicating that Rosalinda should go ahead. She did, and the doctor's wife followed, giving Delbert a bemused glance as she passed. The doctor trudged through a parlor and into a side room that served as his office. He tapped the leather-covered examination table. "Lie the baby down here," he said to Rosalinda.

Undressed, the child was clearly ill, though Delbert was un-
sure how he might know such a thing. The doctor went to
work with hands and stethoscope.

The doctor's wife turned to Rosalinda. "You live on the
river?"

Rosalinda was startled, having expected no direct questions.
"Yes ma'am," she said. "All our lives we been river people."

"I'm so sorry," the doctor's wife murmured.

Delbert was working to fathom the remark — sorry for the
sick child or sorry the Breedloves were river people — when
there was a firm knocking from the front of the house.

"Now what," the doctor said, keeping his attention with the
infant on his table.

"I'll get it, Ed." The doctor's wife slipped away to answer. In
a moment she was back. "Seems to be for you," she said to
Delbert.

"Me?" Delbert offered up his best surprise.

"Yes indeed. The sheriff." She continued her bemused
expression. "Ed," she said to her husband, "sheriff'd like to see
you, too."

The doctor looked up, confused. "The sheriff?"

"Must be that business down at the bank," Delbert said easily. "I might have been a bit hasty in my management of that
situation. Doctor, I could use your assistance on this matter."

The doctor had been hunched over the baby; now he stood
with a face full of misgiving. "Let's go," he said to Delbert.

The two men trailed through the parlor and onto the porch.
Beyond the fence were two cars and about eight men standing
around them, at the ready with shotguns. The doctor looked
out at the battle array.

An old sheriff stood alone on the porch, a respectful short

distance from the doorway. He touched the brim of his hat. "Doc Garnett, how are you? Sorry to bother you like this."

"What the hell's going on?"

"We need that fella behind you there," the sheriff said. "The clown."

Delbert lifted his right hand, the white flag. "Keene's the name, Sheriff. I can shed some light on this problem."

Doctor Garnett stared at Delbert. "What's this all about?"

"Well, sir," Delbert said, "this is what we might call an innocent misunderstanding."

The sheriff said, "This man robbed the Farmers and Merchants not a half-hour ago. We're taking him in."

Delbert ignored the sheriff. "You see, Doctor, the young lady in there with the baby was worried you wouldn't see her if she couldn't pay you, and we couldn't let the baby get worse if it was only a matter of a few dollars —"

"You think I'd let a child die for lack of a fee?"

"Well, I don't know you!" Delbert straightened. "I didn't know what to expect . . ."

"There's a depression going on, in case you haven't noticed, mister," Garnett said. "No physician worth his salt would turn away somebody for lack of money. Not in Tennessee."

Delbert pointed at the doctor. "Don't tell me what people will do, Ed." His voice rose. "The world's a far sight bigger than Tennessee."

The doctor's eyes pulled together. "Don't call me *Ed.*"

"Well, that's your damn name, isn't it? Or your wife just call you that to make fun of you —"

"Hey!" The sheriff stepped across to grab Delbert's arm. "You're under arrest, mister. We got a witness says you robbed the Farmers and Merchants."

Delbert hooted. "Positive identification! Look at this face-paint. Maybe it was *another* clown, you ever think of that, Sheriff?"

Two or three of the shotguns out by the fence were getting restless, stepping closer. The sheriff paused, looking at Delbert and then Doctor Garnett, bewildered. "*Another* clown?"

Garnett shrugged, gazing out at the posse. "He's crazy. That's my opinion. Insane."

Delbert bobbed his head around. "I've heard that before," he said. "It's been a popular opinion in my life."

The doctor did not speak. Mrs. Garnett materialized in the doorway.

"Keep back, ma'am," the sheriff said. "We're taking this man in."

"I didn't rob the bank," Delbert said patiently. "I borrowed some cash to pay Ed here. I'm good for it."

The sheriff told Doctor Garnett this was not the teller's story. "She's got him taking the money right from the cash drawer and running out with it."

"I didn't run out with it," Delbert protested. "I walked."

"You're under arrest," the sheriff said evenly. "I don't know who you are or what your game is, but you're going to jail until we figure it out."

Mrs. Garnett stepped forward onto the porch, speaking to Delbert. "You say you took this money to pay my husband?"

Delbert sighed. "Ma'am, I see now how ridiculous that sounds, but that's the fact of the matter, yes."

"It didn't occur to you to come down here and ask first?"

Delbert was silent as the sheriff put him in handcuffs. He looked down at the cuffs, and back at Mrs. Garnett. "No ma'am," he said. "I suppose in my passion to do a good turn . . . I wasn't thinking too clearly."

"No sir," Mrs. Garnett said, "you certainly were not."

"Get him out of here, Sheriff," the doctor said. "I've got work to do."

"Yes sir," the sheriff said, whirling Delbert away and pushing him toward the porch steps. Delbert stumbled and took natural advantage of the moment to twirl a comical lopsided pirouette down the steps. Mrs. Garnett smiled, and the shotgun posse took her lead and relaxed, standing at ease, leaning on their weapons as if they were hay rakes. At the gate Delbert turned and shouted to the doctor, "Take good care of that little baby, Ed!" But the doctor was gone, inside the house. The sheriff shoved Delbert on along to one of the waiting cars.

At the car door Delbert suddenly drew erect, puffing his chest, inflating his jaws and jutting his chin to render the clownface even more absurd, lifting his head in mockery of any vainglorious politician. "Gentlemen, I thank you for your kind support today, for making sure the sheriff didn't get carried away up there!" The deputies looked at each other, grinning and shaking their heads. "I want you to know I always felt better, knowing you boys were here, watching out for me! Protecting my rights! You boys are part of what makes this country great!"

The sheriff pushed Delbert into the car as the deputies broke into spontaneous applause.

■　■　■

Delbert was arraigned, formally charged and incarcerated in the county jail to await trial. The sheriff brought a pail of water into his cell, instructed Delbert to wash the paint from his face and banged out. A cape of sparrows flocked past his cell window. There were the sounds of children playing in a peaceful distance. Standing against the wall of his cell and looking out

Delbert could see the branching shapes of trees in full mid-summer leaf, and he remembered the moment in Faulk's car with Rosalinda Breedlove as he turned his neck to look up at the trees soaring above them. The trees nearly covered the sky, their pure reach seeming to Delbert a fortunate grace, an accidental power and beauty. Like a summer river, he had told her. As if she would know what he was talking about. Or, he thought, she did, she knew exactly what he was talking about, she knew all too well.

PART III

1

LATE IN THE DAY of his arrest Delbert received a paper sack
at the jail with a few of his circus belongings. Faulk had
penned a note and dropped it into the bag: YOU ARE FIRED.
JF. Meal plates were carried in from a nearby restaurant, better
fare than what was served out of the Raney Brothers pie car.
Delbert ate happily, finding his cell in Hornbeak to be far from
the worst place he had ever landed. He pulled the steel-frame
cot under his window so he could stand and look out. A deputy came in the morning to empty the chamberpot.

"Quite some little town you got here," Delbert said from the
window.

The deputy sloshed Delbert's waste into a bucket. "Nothing
much for a town," he said.

Delbert nestled his chin against his hands, surveying what
he could see of the summer morning through the bars: a bare
alley opening into the doorway of a garage. Somebody moved
about inside the garage in deep shadow. "Now don't talk that
way," Delbert murmured. "A man's town is his castle."

The deputy looked up from his chore but said nothing, and

let himself out of the cell. In a few minutes the sheriff came into the cell block with the jangling authority of his key ring announcing the entry. Delbert didn't look around.

"Keene!" The sheriff was vested in power and proud of it. "Man here to see you."

"Sure is a lovely morning," Delbert called from the window.

"Get the hell down from there! I said there's a man here to see you."

Delbert turned to see a small man standing beside the sheriff, fastidious behind rimless glasses, balding, in a three-piece pinstripe suit. Delbert whistled softly looking at the man, dropped off his bunk and went to the cell door, extending his right hand through the bars. "My, my," Delbert said, "you're just neat as a pin."

The man in the suit accepted Delbert's handshake.

"Let me guess," Delbert said. "Bank president? Well, sir, you should've got back every red cent. I handed it over to the sheriff here."

"I'll leave you now," the sheriff said to the man in the suit. "Holler if this monkey gets out of hand."

Delbert watched the sheriff go, and the small man cleared his throat. "Mr. Keene, I'm Hayward Fleming. I'm a lawyer." Fleming spoke in the flattened jew's-harp tones of the mountain-bred.

"Lawyer! Excuse me, sir!" Delbert shook his head. "My apologies. Lawyer, banker . . ."

"I've been appointed by the court to look into this matter of the incident down at Farmers and Merchants."

"Well, pull up a chair," Delbert said, as if the two men were in a parlor. "I believe there's a seat out there."

Fleming glanced around to find a chair left by the night

deputy, who had shared several shots of bourbon with Delbert the evening before, after Delbert had gone into large detail about his sister who had been out hunting and nearly shot her husband, mistaking him for wild game.

Fleming inspected the cane seat of the chair, which seemed about to give way. "Not to worry," Delbert said. "It held a man up for hours last night."

Fleming sat, drawing notebook and pen from an inside breast pocket. Then he stared a moment at Delbert.

Delbert gripped the two bars on either side of his head, leaning his face into the space between his arms. His eyes were wide, faultless and pristine.

"Mr. Keene," Fleming said at length, "I'm advised that you went into that bank lobby with your face painted as a clown."

"Well, I *am* a clown. That's my profession." Delbert grinned. "Humble though it may be."

"Surely you might have suspected such a get-up could alarm somebody?"

"Alarm somebody? Who's afraid of a clown?"

Fleming shifted carefully on the chair. "What I mean is, a clown belongs in a circus, not in a bank lobby. Or a doctor's office."

Delbert launched backward from the bars to land sitting on the edge of his bunk. "I'll wager you're unaware of how long it takes a working clown to put on a decent face. Or take one off."

"Why don't you clue me in, Mr. Keene."

"I simply did not have time to take off the face. Not if I was to lend a helping hand to the lady in need."

Fleming nodded, maintaining an expression devoid of any possibility. "Okay. What about this lady?"

Delbert told Fleming how he had seen Rosalinda Breedlove afoot on the perimeter of the circus grounds with a baby in her arms, that he had taken pity and looked to help out.

"So you stole" — here Fleming referred to his notebook — "an automobile owned by one James Faulk."

Delbert held his hands aloft, rippling his fingers in the air. "You hear anything about my concertina?" he asked. "It was among my effects back at the circus."

"No sir." Fleming paused. "Mr. Keene, the car? Faulk's Chevy?"

"Borrowed," Delbert announced firmly. "Why the hell should I *steal* his damned car?"

"Why the hell should you?"

Delbert looked to one side. "You know, Jimmy Faulk's a disappointment. Not standing behind me on this thing."

Fleming dropped notebook and pen in his lap and covered them with his hands. "You make it hard for anybody to stand by you. You run off with another man's car, wearing a disguise, pick up some woman nobody's ever heard of, and rob a bank. You're a regular Bonnie and Clyde."

"That was *not* a disguise! I explained that, and may I say I explained it *carefully*, to that little dimwit in the bank."

Fleming wagged a finger. "She was scared to death, you know that, mister? She thought you were gonna shoot her!"

Delbert waved, dismissing the idea. "Like hell she did. You believe that you'll go for anything."

Fleming was again silent for a moment, collecting himself. "If I believe *you* I'll go for anything."

Delbert shuffled to one wall of the cell, arms folded, exhaling. "It happened like I said, Hayward." He set his gaze seriously at Fleming. "You got a sworn duty to get me out of here. Do I count on you?"

"Oh hell!" Fleming rammed notebook and pen back into a pocket, and stood. "You got any questions?"

Delbert moved to the center of the cell, stroking his chin, a portrait of contemplation. "Well, sir, I do. I've never got a satisfactory answer to this one either."

"What the hell is it?"

"On what side of a house does an oak tree grow?"

"Jesus Christ!" Fleming went to the cell-block door and pounded on it. "Sheriff! Get me out of here!"

Delbert lifted his arms, self-deprecating.

The cell-block door clanged open; Fleming moved past the sheriff and out without a word as Delbert squeezed his face between two bars to shout, "Remember your sworn duty, Hayward!"

2

Delbert read the account in the *Hornbeak Weekly Sentinel* of a thirty-five-year-old man who, disguised as a circus clown, stole a car and later duped a bank teller into parting with $200, allegedly to pay an indigent young mother's doctor bill.

The nightshift deputy who brought Delbert the newspaper sat on the cane chair working at his gums with a toothpick. "How about that?" The deputy turned to spit on the floor. "You're good as convicted, I'd say."

Delbert folded the newspaper neatly. "You mind if I keep this?"

The deputy shrugged, and Delbert slid the paper under his pillow.

"Yessir," the deputy drawled, cocking the chair back on two legs, "you're as good as up the river."

Delbert lay back on his cot. "You're forgetting that I'm represented by none other than Hayward Fleming himself. A regular wizard of the courtroom, I'm told."

"Yeah? I wonder who might have told you that?"

"Besides," Delbert said, "an upstanding jury of the good

people of Hornbeak will see that this is all a gigantic misunderstanding."

The deputy was confused. "They will?"

"Try to help somebody out, look what happens," Delbert mused. He turned his head on the pillow to look at the deputy. "I probably *am* crazy, you know that?"

The deputy let his chair fall forward. "You are?"

"Just try and do a simple good turn." Delbert was gazing at the ceiling again.

"You care for a touch of refreshment?"

"You know, brother, I believe I could stand just something like that. Medicinal purposes only, of course."

3

Rainmaker coming, yes indeed. Rainmaker on the way with no other name but one, no other place to go except where you are, where you wait looking up an empty road to see him coming on foot of a late summer's afternoon. Watch for him in your hills, in your town, right out there behind your house, standing in your kitchen, in a corner of your bedroom looking every way at once, the man with the sky in his pocket. Because bringing the rain is an old and honored profession, let me tell you. Rainmaker was here with Jesus and Hannibal, he served the Greek kings, the lost tribes of Africa, the dreamers of Zanzibar, anyone else you can think of. Rainmaker always comes when he's called.

Delbert remembered the story from his cell in Hornbeak, one of the stories he told children gathered around his wagon before and after the tent shows, watching him putting on his clown's facepaint or taking it off, asking how he could make people laugh like it was easy. He looked around at the pitched faces already tired as their exhausted parents' faces, the desperation pressed flat against bones and eyes the color of water.

One in the group, usually a boy, asked how to call up a rainmaker.

"You just think about him," Delbert said. "You look up into that dry old sky hoping for the sound and the smell of rain, and you try your level best to see the Rainmaker's face in the shapes of the clouds. Pretty soon here he comes and when he comes you look at him and he never looks the same way twice. Rainmaker comes to your mama's back door looking for bread and a single day's work, that's one way you might recognize him. He'll hitch a ride all the way to town and then you don't see him no more. He might appear to be someone else, blacksmith, farmer. Circus clown. Never can tell."

The children huddled in the doorway of the wagon, staring intently at Delbert. None of them spoke. Across the pasture, a cow elephant with a sequined headdress stood with a ball and chain on her left front foot.

Delbert leaned back in his chair. "Never can tell," he said.

■ ■ ■

One story he always told at night, after the last show. "You all ever hear about the Skin Spinner?" Delbert asked the question flat-eyed. And a child inside every group would say *A what?*

"Skin Spinner," Delbert said. "Very strange. Situation that happened to my brother, actually."

Delbert would pause. And the children waited.

"Seems that my brother knew of a woman who could spin her skin right off her body, spin it right onto a spinning wheel and fit herself into the skin of a cat, go out all night and prowl, eat things alive. You ever wonder how it might be to live inside the skin of another creature, walking like that creature, eating what it eats, talking the same way? Well, this was a woman who knew what all that was like. She'd come home of a morning, spin that skin back onto her body, sweet as can be, nobody the wiser. Except my brother, of course."

"You say you knew this woman?"

"I said my brother knew this lady. Point of fact, he was married to her." Delbert looked around the group, moving his eyes from face to face. "Yes indeed," he continued, "the lady in question happened to be my sister-in-law."

"You ever see her do this spinning thing?"

"God, no! Happily not. But my poor brother did. 'Course when he got married to her he didn't know a thing about what she did after the sun went down. He didn't discover that part for a while. And when he did, don't you know he was as gone as a man can get. He packed his bags and lit out and by the time he told me the story he hadn't seen or heard of his wife for some little time. Which was fine by him."

The children looked at each other, and Delbert said, "I tell you this story only because I heard it from my brother. So that's getting it on the best authority."

Silence stood among the children a moment; then one or two began to giggle. With that the group erupted in laughter. Delbert laughed with them, his hands suddenly in the air and the children's laughter rising away, into the night, dispelling demons and a clown's fine tale as Delbert said, "It's true! Every word of it!"

The children laughed harder and Delbert called out, "A man's brother wouldn't lie to him, would he?"

∎　∎　∎

Hayward Fleming stood at the bars of Delbert's cell, gazing in mournfully at his client, who was doing a handstand in one corner, resting his sock feet against the wall.

"You ought to give this a try, Hayward," Delbert said. "Runs a little blood into the brain. Refreshes the thought process."

"Maybe you should have tried it before you ran off with that girl."

"My damsel in distress?" Delbert's face was reddening.

"The damsel nobody can find."

Delbert let his feet fall forward, bringing himself cleanly into an upright crouch. From that position he regarded Fleming.

"Doc says he never saw her before, your damsel."

"So what?"

"Mr. Keene, a person you can't find is a person who can't testify."

Delbert began to hum "The Old Rugged Cross."

"There's another problem, too," Fleming said.

Delbert cut short with his humming and stood. "You know, it don't reassure me having you discover problems all the time. You're supposed to be working this all out for me."

"The other problem," Fleming continued, "is that one way or another the word got out about your little escapade."

Delbert moved to the cot and sat down at one end, folding his hands in his lap.

"There's a newspaper boy right outside waiting to get in here." Fleming bit at his upper lip before he continued. "He's from Memphis."

"Memphis!" Delbert threw open his arms in welcome. "Send him in!"

"Don't be so damned happy," Fleming said. "All it does is make matters worse."

"Why? Now everybody in Memphis'll know I'm an innocent man."

Fleming looked at his shoes. "Trial's in three days."

Delbert said, "Send in that fella from Memphis. Maybe he brought me a present."

4

The newspaperman was young, bright-eyed in a rumpled blue serge suit. He introduced himself as Conway of the *Memphis Commercial Appeal* and explained that the story of Keno the Clown had been picked up by a watchful soul with a wire service and run all over the country. "I'm probably just the first to get here," he said, sitting on the deputy's cane chair.

Delbert had pulled the cot to the bars so he could sit closer to his visitor. "Now that's the damnedest thing," he said.

"Not really. Human interest. First-class human interest." Conway's blond hair was thinning despite his youth, and was combed back to highlight a fierce widow's peak. "So I'm here to find out all about a circus clown named Keno."

Delbert smiled. "Happy to oblige."

"My taking notes won't bother you?"

"All the better," Delbert said. "The memory's a poor second, am I right?"

Conway glanced up from what he was writing. "Right," he said, and launched into a line of background questions: where Delbert was born, his age, how he came to be a clown. Delbert answered the questions at length, improvising veracity, embroidering fresh happenstance as the moment inspired him. When Conway got to the events surrounding Rosalinda Breedlove, Delbert stayed closer to the absolute truth, realizing as he spoke that the events themselves needed little assistance. Conway confirmed Delbert's personal belief that no crime had been committed at any point in the efforts to bring care and comfort to a sick child, and grinned over his notes.

"What do you think?" Delbert asked.

"Well, Keno, I think you're a hero. We got us a great story here."

Keno, I think you're a hero. Nodding with satisfaction, Delbert lay back on the cot, hands tucked behind his head, wishing for his concertina.

■　■　■

Conway had been correct: newsmen paraded past Delbert, from the *Nashville Tennessean, Atlanta Journal, Louisville Times.* Most of the reporters were younger than Delbert, of decidedly different personal histories and private inclinations, college educated, with inheritances and complicated politics. The *Hornbeak Weekly Sentinel* reported on the reporters as if they were visiting film stars and Hayward Fleming asked the judge to sequester Delbert in the interest of a nonpartisan proceeding. The request was granted. The last journalist Delbert saw was an overweight Jewish boy from the *Richmond News Leader.* Delbert asked to borrow a sheet of paper from the reporter's notebook, and his pencil, and wrote to Elsie and the children: *I am fine. All is well. Not to worry. Kids when you are old enough you can come with me to the circus. Big time then. Del.* Folding once, Delbert wrote the address on the overleaf and asked the reporter from Richmond to see that the note was mailed.

Alone in his cell the night before the trial it occurred to Delbert that certain aspects of his life were perhaps ranging out of control, that the notions of will and choice had become prisoners of any given moment. He imagined Elsie opening his note in a week's time, maybe showing it to the kids, maybe not. In the few years since Wilson Stinchcomb had picked him up on the highway Delbert had not forgotten his family; he sent decorated cards to the children, short notes written to Elsie on the back of Wa-hoo Bitters handbills. From time to time he folded a twenty-dollar bill into an envelope, sending it off in the sure knowledge that he was a man of no fixed address.

It was not unusual for the better part of a bottle to go down on the night of mailing such a letter — Delbert's own rite of everyday grief, his ritual observance of the uncertain vagrancies of spirit in what had never come to pass. After midnight, in solemn stupor and the bottle half done, Delbert remembered summer nights in the bedroom of his family home in Boaz, the hot dark air a ceremony of small voices fighting for a chance at sleep. His sister Louise would wake him quietly and take him to the porch where they could eat the candy she had been given earlier in the day by the storekeeper — only enough for the two of them. Hard candy, rainbow colors; Delbert could summon the taste in his mouth, sweet as whiskey after all those years. Louise always remembered him. Silent Louise. Delbert was once in the sliding house of such a memory, his face wet with tears, when Wilson Stinchcomb discovered him. Wilson sat down beside him. *I'll be okay here in a minute*, Delbert had said.

No you won't, Wilson told him. *You've never been okay and you never will be.*

"Well," Delbert said aloud in his cell, "maybe not." He stood on his cot to look out into the night — the garage behind the jail was brightly lit, a big happy glare of white light filling out a room of workbenches and racked tools. There was a worse-for-wear Model T in the bay.

"Hello there!" Delbert shouted. "Top of the evening to you!"

No answer, no sign of movement inside.

"Anybody home?" Delbert called.

The car sat low on its tires. Nobody heeded Delbert's greeting. The garage was like a circus tent before the audience arrived: clean and invulnerable, with the best light history can buy. Delbert tried to get this idea across to Hayward Fleming the next morning in the courtroom. Fleming shuffled pages, wrote notes to himself. Delbert leaned over and said, "This courtroom's probably no different. You ever sit in here before the show starts?"

Fleming looked at Delbert, and said, "This is not a show, Mr. Keene. I'd like you to get hold of that idea."

Delbert repositioned in his chair. "Just a manner of speaking, Hayward."

"And when you're on the stand, call me Mr. Fleming."

"By the way, Hayward, I never did get an answer to my question."

Fleming sighed. "What question was that?"

Delbert shook his head, a show of disappointment. "How soon we forget," he said. "My question was, on what side of a house does an oak tree grow?"

Fleming stared sad-eyed at his client. Delbert grinned, and said, "The *outside,* Hayward."

The bailiff had everybody rise as the judge, a portly man swimming in judicial robes, came into the courtroom. After all returned to their seats Delbert offered a friendly wave to judge and jury. The judge directed a brief clinical inspection toward Delbert and slammed his gavel, bringing the proceedings to order.

5

Doctor Edward Garnett was first on the stand in the prosecution's behalf. He was taciturn. Yes, a man looking like a circus clown had presented at his home and office seven days earlier, delivering a young woman and an admittedly sick infant. Garnett had cared for the infant, who would do fine, he thought. He did not know the baby's mother, having never seen her before or since.

"Doctor, could you point out the man who came to your home? Is he in the courtroom?"

"Well," Garnett said, "I assume that's him over there next to Mr. Fleming."

"You assume?"

Garnett looked directly at the prosecutor. "That's right," he said. "I assume."

The doctor avoided a psychiatric opinion when pressed for it, telling the court it was out of his line. The prosecution called Miss Virginia Lembard, bank teller at the Farmers and Merchants of Hornbeak.

Miss Lembard conducted herself as she had the day Delbert

had last seen her, with the dour caution of a perennially un-
dermined soul. She described in low tones how a man had
entered the bank in a suit with no necktie and his face all
painted like a clown. The judge had to ask her to speak up.
She turned to the judge as if he had insulted her, and cleared
her throat.

The prosecutor asked her to point this man out in the courtroom, if she saw him.

"I don't know if he's in here."

"You don't recognize this man you've told us about?"

"Well," she said, "his face was *painted*."

The prosecutor appeared to be unprepared for this obvious
point. "Miss Lembard," he said after a hesitation, "was there
anything about this man by which you could identify him?"

"I don't know." Miss Lembard was petulant. "Maybe by his
talk. He had a funny way of talking."

"A funny way of talking?"

"You know, it was . . . different."

The prosecutor stroked his moustache, glancing around at
the table where Delbert and Hayward Fleming sat side by side.
Delbert was enjoying the proceedings, smiling at the prosecutor. "Could you tell us all exactly what you mean, ma'am?
You mean he made you laugh?"

"No!" The gust of her own single word seemed to frighten
Miss Lembard. She looked wide-eyed at the jury.

The prosecutor stepped away from the witness box. "Go on,
please."

"It's that his voice was . . . sweet. I mean, he talked good,
used words like they was strung together somehow."

Delbert suddenly spoke from his spot next to Fleming.
"We'll find the poet in Miss Lembard yet!"

The judge clapped his gavel, directing a stern glare toward Delbert. "I'll have order, sir. You'll speak when I tell you to, not before."

Delbert took a long breath before he responded. "Sorry," he said.

The prosecutor continued. "So you mean he had a *style* of speaking?"

"I guess."

At this point the judge intervened to ask the prosecutor if his inquiry was pointed anywhere in particular.

"Sir, I'm trying to get at a way of establishing identity for the man who seems to have robbed a bank in this town."

"I'm well aware of your intentions, Mr. Wilk. But I'm not at all sure that having Miss Lembard listen to a line of people talk to her will be all that convincing."

The prosecutor stalked back to his chair, speaking as he moved. "Perhaps Your Honor has a better idea?"

The judge looked at Delbert. "Why don't we just ask the man in question?"

Hayward Fleming turned to Delbert, rolling a pencil between thumb and forefinger. Then he stood. "Your Honor, isn't this a bit irregular?"

The judge snorted. "It sure is. But I'll bet we could save us ne time. As it is, your boy's had a story for every newspaper _ween here and Pittsburgh. And if he'll talk to them, maybe he'll talk to us."

"Happy to oblige, Your Honor," Delbert called forth.

Fleming looked down at Delbert. "Will you kindly shut up?"

■　■　■

Delbert was examined and cross-examined, recounting his story, answering the prosecutor's questions, parlaying the moment with frequent asides to the jury.

"Has nobody here had the impulse to help another soul?" Delbert's voice rolled in address to the courtroom gallery.

"I'm sure we all have, Mr. Keene," Fleming said, "but we're talking about you, your situation."

Delbert considered Fleming a moment before turning to the judge and asking permission to address the jury himself. Both attorneys immediately objected.

"Sir, that's not the usual way a courtroom operates," the judge said.

"Well, Your Honor," Delbert said, "it's just that these two lawyers here have just about run out of gas, if I'm not mistaken."

The judge could not conceal his amusement. Fleming returned to his seat, defeated. Wilk offered a second objection.

"Overruled," the judge said. "Mr. Keene, please keep your remarks brief."

"Thank you, sir." Delbert turned to the jury, then back to the judge. "May I get out of this box, Your Honor?"

"I suppose so."

Delbert stepped down and moved to face the jury. "I just thought I could get to the bottom of this for you, get right down to the heart of the matter. Because, folks, this is all what you might call one big accident. All I cared to do was help out a woman and a sick baby, speed them both along to a little bit of assistance. Now it's become apparent that I might have made a few mistakes along the way, maybe mishandled a few things here and there and that . . . well, that I might have been misunderstood. God knows, that's been my story in this life —"

"Mr. Keene," the judge murmured.

"Ah, yes sir," Delbert said, nodding. "I'll keep on track here."

"Thank you, sir."

Delbert recalled a photograph he had once seen of Clarence Darrow. He put his hands on the balustrade that bordered the jury box, leaning intently, doing his best imitation. "What all you folks should know is simple enough: everything came out, the baby got the attention it needed and the bank didn't lose a penny. So maybe I'm a crazy man who needs put away for the good of society. I'm clearly not qualified to say. I'm just going to put my fate in your hands. I'll just go back across the street to my jail cell and wait to hear from you good people."

A spatter of handclapping circled around the courtroom.

The judge brought down his gavel one time.

■ ■ ■

Returned to his cell, Delbert lay on the cot. For the first time since arriving in Hornbeak, Tennessee, he felt a heat lightning of regret flickering near the base of his skull. A man can have a good time, but enough is enough: when the adventure's run its course you take a bow and head back to where you came from. Delbert had always worked by this principle, but the jurors' faces betrayed nothing. Two rheumy-eyed farm wives, the rest old men who'd been bitten once too often by their horses. A fine array of sallow cheeks and black teeth. Not one of them, Delbert imagined, could tell a good joke or remember the day they'd had enough to live on. No one among them had even so much as walked fast in the last fifteen years. "What a goddamn country," Delbert said to the ceiling.

He lay there, imagining himself an old man, thinking he might not look far different from some of the faces in the jury: a wicket of ear hair, arbor of broken veins rising across his upper lip and nose, eyes faded to gray on the mileage they'd spawned — the blight of too many winter storms and every old man's cold fire. He'd still be surviving on the memory of one fine love, the single true thing that could account for its own distance.

Delbert whispered to himself: *You ever hear the story of the Rainmaker? Well let me tell you. Rainmaker's on the way, oh my yes, coming to your town to damn well wash it away. Wash it straight to kingdom come. Wash away your sins, one and all.* He thought he heard a noise in the alley behind the jail and stood on the cot for a look.

The garage that had been lush in its burgeoning light the night before was closed, a dilapidated wooden door pulled across the entrance and padlocked.

"Well," Delbert said, "goodbye to you, too."

6

"They're ready for you, Keene." The sheriff unlocked the cell door.

"Couldn't be more than an hour," Delbert remarked.

"Let's go."

Delbert moved to the open door. "Maybe a good sign, not taking too long to make up their minds."

The sheriff shrugged. "I got no idea. Seen a jury take as little as fifteen minutes to send a man to the gallows. You never know."

Delbert smiled. "Those are encouraging words, Sheriff. I thank you."

The sheriff walked behind Delbert, out of the jailhouse and across the street, into the courthouse. Delbert moved up the center aisle to take his place next to Hayward Fleming.

Fleming made no eye contact. The judge directed the bailiff to call in the jury. Delbert leaned toward Fleming, whispering in his ear: "Hayward, you learn anything from how I spoke to the jury?"

Fleming stared straight ahead.

"Perhaps you might want to adopt a more personal manner," Delbert whispered.

Fleming sighed as the jury resumed its place. The judge asked if a decision had been reached, and the old farmer selected as foreman rose from his chair to say they had one, sure enough.

"John," the judge said to the foreman, "share it with us, if you would."

The foreman looked across at Delbert. "We figure him for not guilty."

Several of the newspaper reporters immediately left the courtroom. There was a murmur of approval.

The judge turned his attention to Delbert. "Mr. Keene?"

"Yes sir?"

"Would you stand up?"

Delbert did so.

The judge leveled a practiced paternal gaze. "You're acquitted, Mr. Keene. Which is the sensible thing to do in this ridiculous matter. I'm going to ask the sheriff to escort you to the city limits at first opportunity."

Delbert said it would be his pleasure.

"Ours too," said the judge.

■   ■   ■

Delbert hitchhiked south, following a trail of rain-soaked handbills nailed to telephone poles along State Highway 45 to find the circus playing a weekend stand outside Corinth, Mississippi. He pounded on the door of Hud Raney's wagon just before dusk. When Raney opened the door Delbert said, "Sure is a lovely evening."

Raney stared a moment. "You know, Jimmy Faulk's about ready to kill you."

Delbert looked around, feigning a search for Faulk. "I'm prepared to apologize. Where is he?"

Raney stood away from the door, gesturing Delbert inside. "You better get in here, before he sees you."

Delbert accepted a seat on a campstool, announcing he had been declared an innocent man by the fair people of Hornbeak.

Raney sat opposite Delbert on a trunk lid. "Keno, why didn't you just ask Faulk for the car?"

"He would've said no and you know it."

"And if he did you should've just left well enough alone."

"Well, now, Hud, that's the problem. Leave well enough alone and nobody does anything."

Raney looked as if he had bitten into bad fruit.

"You can't disagree with me on that," Delbert said.

Raney said he could smooth it over with Faulk. "What was that about a bank robbery? Did you do that? I couldn't believe it when I read it."

Delbert was impressed. "You read it?"

"Hell, yes," Raney said. "It was in a newspaper up in Jackson."

"You save that particular issue?"

Raney laughed. "As a matter of fact I did tuck it away somewhere. You keeping a scrapbook?"

Delbert lifted his eyebrows. "There's an idea! I hadn't thought of that. Little something for the kids."

Raney studied Delbert. "Keno, did you rob that bank?"

"Pure misunderstanding," Delbert said. "I went in for a loan, you understand, so I could pay the doctor I was taking that baby to see."

"You asked for a *loan?*"

Delbert shrugged. "You get a loan at a bank, right?"

Raney shook his head. "Keno, you know your fundamental trouble? You never know when the show's over."

From where he sat Delbert could see through the tiny window to the circus grounds: one of the white parade ponies ambled past, majestic in sequins. Beyond, the big-top curved down out of the sky's falling light. Delbert watched the scene a moment before he asked Raney if Tressa Sinclair was still in the show.

Raney nodded. "Sure is."

"Now there's a lady that walked out of a dream if there ever was one," Delbert said. "She handles that trapeze like it's all silk up there."

"She's a good one, no doubt about it."

"She really looks like she's on a pair of wings, you know that, Hud?" Delbert turned his face skyward, in the grip of his vision. "As if she can fly and the rest of us are glued in the mud."

Raney was silent. Delbert brought his gaze back into the wagon and said, "I believe I'm in love with that woman."

"Jesus Christ, Keno." Raney pushed a hand through his hair. "You going to go to work tonight? Or sit here daydreaming about Tressa Sinclair?"

Delbert looked at Raney as if he had not heard. "Hud, you still got my concertina, don't you?"

7

Delbert was in the circus that night, madcap, the glint of passing smiles as he lurched past crowded stands, rolling with Raney's other two clowns. They brained each other with huge rubber hammers, and Delbert had his partners stare curiously into the muzzle of a miniature cannon as he lit the dead-end wick and grinned maniacally at the squealing audience. With a sparkling troupe of equestrians prepared to enter, Delbert threw a last pratfall at the edge of the crowd's attention and vaulted away from the ring to trot out of the big-top in his floral regalia: whiteface under an orange wig, red bulb nose and crescent-moon eyebrows, slapping jester's shoes. He walked into the slow heat of midsummer in Mississippi, trees shadowing beyond the animal pens, and squatted in a patch of bluegrass among the circled vans to listen to the shape of the wind as it rode the night in open country. Alone — the crowd's roar inside the tent like a distant dream — Delbert sat and watched the shape of the land rising into its own long sleep, imagining the wind was the sound of a single desire and that, listening to it, he might live forever.

ABOUT THE AUTHOR

Richard Currey's first novel, *Fatal Light,* was accorded a Special Citation from the Ernest Hemingway Foundation, won the Vietnam Veterans of America's Excellence in the Arts Award, and has been published in ten languages. His stories have appeared in *Best American Short Stories, Prize Stories 1988: The O. Henry Awards, New American Short Stories,* and *NRF,* France's most prestigious literary magazine. A native of Wood County, West Virginia, he now lives with his family in New Mexico.